WHERE THERE'S A WILL

BY MARY ROBERTS RINEHART

TABLE OF CONTENTS

CHAPTER I

I HAVE A WARNING

When it was all over Mr. Sam came out to the spring-house to say good-by to me before he and Mrs. Sam left. I hated to see him go, after all we had been through together, and I suppose he saw it in my face, for he came over close and stood looking down at me, and smiling. "You saved us, Minnie," he said, "and I needn't tell you we're grateful; but do you know what I think?" he asked, pointing his long forefinger at me. "I think you've enjoyed it even when you were suffering most. Red-haired women are born to intrigue, as the sparks fly upward."

"Enjoyed it!" I snapped. "I'm an old woman before my time, Mr. Sam. What with trailing back and forward through the snow to the shelter-house, and not getting to bed at all some nights, and my heart going by fits and starts, as you may say, and half the time my spinal marrow fairly chilled—not to mention putting on my overshoes every morning from force of habit and having to take them off again, I'm about all in."

"It's been the making of you, Minnie," he said, eying me, with his hands in his pockets. "Look at your cheeks! Look at your disposition! I don't believe you'd stab anybody in the back now!"

Which was a joke, of course; I never stabbed anybody in the back.

He sauntered over and dropped a quarter into the slot-machine by the door, but the thing was frozen up and refused to work. I've seen the time when Mr. Sam would have kicked it, but he merely looked at it and then at me.

"Turned virtuous, like everything else around the place. Not that I don't approve of virtue, Minnie, but I haven't got used to putting my foot on the brass rail of the bar and ordering a nut sundae. Hook the money out with a hairpin, Minnie, and buy some shredded wheat in remembrance of me."

He opened the door and a blast of February wind rattled the window-frames. Mr. Sam threw out his chest under his sweater and waved me another good-by.

"Well, I'm off, Minnie," he said. "Take care of yourself and don't sit too tight on the job; learn to rise a bit in the saddle."

"Good-by, Mr. Sam!" I called, putting down Miss Patty's doily and following him to the door; "good-by; better have something before you start to keep you warm."

He turned at the corner of the path and grinned back at me.

"All right," he called. "I'll go down to the bar and get a lettuce sandwich!"

Then he was gone, and happy as I was, I knew I would miss him terribly. I got a wire hairpin and went over to the slot-machine, but when I had finally dug out the money I could hardly see it for tears.

It began when the old doctor died. I suppose you have heard of Hope Sanatorium and the mineral spring that made it famous. Perhaps you have seen the blotter we got out, with a flash-light interior of the spring-house on it, and me handing the old doctor a glass of mineral water, and wearing the embroidered linen waist that Miss Patty Jennings gave me that winter. The blotters were a great success. Below the picture it said, "Yours for health," and in the body of the blotter, in red lettering, "Your system absorbs the health-giving drugs in Hope Springs water as this blotter soaks up ink."

The "Yours for health" was my idea.

I have been spring-house girl at Hope Springs Sanatorium for fourteen years. My father had the position before me, but he took rheumatism, and as the old doctor said, it was bad business policy to spend thousands of dollars in advertising that Hope Springs water cured rheumatism, and then have father creaking like a rusty hinge every time he bent over to fill a glass with it.

Father gave me one piece of advice the day he turned the spring-house over to me.

"It's a difficult situation, my girl," he said. "Lots of people think it's simply a matter of filling a glass with water and handing it over the railing. Why, I tell you a barkeeper's a high-priced man mostly, and his job's a snap to this. I'd like to know how a barkeeper would make out if his customers came back only once a year and he had to remember whether they wanted their drinks cold or hot or 'chill off'. And another thing: if a chap comes in with a tale of woe, does the barkeeper have to ask him what he's doing for it, and listen while he tells how much weight he lost in a blanket sweat? No, sir; he pushes him a bottle and lets it go at that."

Father passed away the following winter. He'd been a little bit delirious, and his last words were: "Yes, sir; hot, with a pinch of salt, sir?" Poor father! The spring had been his career, you may say, and I like to think that perhaps even now he is sitting by some everlasting spring measuring out water with a golden goblet instead of the old tin dipper. I said that to Mr. Sam once, and he said he felt quite sure that I was right, and that where father was the water would be appreciated. He had heard of father.

Well, for the first year or so I nearly went crazy. Then I found things were coming my way. I've got the kind of mind that never forgets a name or face and can combine them properly, which isn't common. And when folks came back I could call them at once. It would do your heart good to see some politician, coming up to rest his stomach from the free bar in the state house at the capital, enter the spring-house where everybody is playing cards and drinking water and not caring a rap whether he's the man that cleans the windows or the secretary of the navy. If he's been there before, in sixty seconds I have his name on my tongue and a glass of water in his hand, and have asked him about the rheumatism in his right knee and how the children are. And in ten minutes he's sitting in a bridge game and trotting to the spring to have his glass refilled during his dummy hand, as if he'd grown up in the place. The old doctor used to say my memory was an asset to the sanatorium.

He depended on me a good bit—the old doctor did—and that winter he was pretty feeble. He was only seventy, but he'd got in the habit of making it eighty to show that the mineral water kept him young. Finally he got to BEING eighty, from thinking it, and he died of senility in the end.

He was in the habit of coming to the spring-house every day to get his morning glass of water and read the papers. For a good many years it had been his custom to sit there, in the winter by the wood fire and in the summer just inside the open door, and to read off the headings aloud while I cleaned around the spring and polished glasses.

"I see the president is going fishing, Minnie," he'd say, or "Airbrake is up to 133; I wish I'd bought it that time I dreamed about it. It was you who persuaded me not to, Minnie."

And all that winter, with the papers full of rumors that Miss Patty Jennings was going to marry a prince, we'd followed it by the spring-house fire, the old doctor and I, getting angry at the Austrian emperor for opposing it when we knew how much too good Miss Patty was for any foreigner, and then getting nervous and fussed when we read that the prince's mother was in favor of the match and it might go through. Miss Patty and her father came every winter to Hope Springs and I couldn't have been more anxious about it if she had been my own sister.

Well, as I say, it all began the very day the old doctor died. He stamped out to the spring-house with the morning paper about nine o'clock, and the wedding seemed to be all off. The paper said the emperor had definitely refused his consent and had sent the prince, who was his cousin, for a Japanese cruise, while the Jennings family was going to Mexico in their private car. The old doctor was indignant, and I remember how he tramped up and down the spring-house, muttering that the girl had had a lucky escape, and what did the emperor expect if beauty and youth and wealth weren't enough. But he calmed down, and soon he was reading that the papers were predicting an early spring, and he said we'd better begin to increase our sulphur percentage in the water.

I hadn't noticed anything strange in his manner, although we'd all noticed how feeble he was growing, but when he got up to go back to the sanatorium and I reached him his cane, it seemed to me he avoided looking at me. He went to the door and then turned and spoke to me over his shoulder.

"By the way," he remarked, "Mr. Richard will be along in a day or so, Minnie. You'd better break it to Mrs. Wiggins."

Since the summer before we'd had to break Mr. Dick's coming to Mrs. Wiggins the housekeeper, owing to his finding her false front where it had blown out of a window, having been hung up to dry, and his wearing it to luncheon as whiskers. Mr. Dick was the old doctor's grandson.

"Humph!" I said, and he turned around and looked square at me.

"He's a good boy at heart, Minnie," he said. "We've had our troubles with him, you and I, but everything has been quiet lately."

When I didn't say anything he looked discouraged, but he had a fine way of keeping on until he gained his point, had the old doctor.

"It HAS been quiet, hasn't it?" he demanded.

"I don't know," I said; "I have been deaf since the last explosion!" And I went down the steps to the spring. I heard the tap of his cane as he came across the floor, and I knew he was angry.

"Confound you, Minnie," he exclaimed, "if I could get along without you I'd discharge you this minute."

"And if I paid any attention to your discharging me I'd have been gone a dozen times in the last year," I retorted. "I'm not objecting to Mr. Dick coming here, am I? Only don't expect me to burst into song about it. Shut the door behind you when you go out."

But he didn't go at once. He stood watching me polish glasses and get the card-tables ready, and I knew he still had something on his mind.

"Minnie," he said at last, "you're a shrewd young woman—maybe more head than heart, but that's well enough. And with your temper under control, you're a CAPABLE young woman."

"What has Mr. Dick been up to now?" I asked, growing suspicious.

"Nothing. But I'm an old man, Minnie, a very old man."

"Stuff and nonsense," I exclaimed, alarmed. "You're only seventy. That's what comes of saying in the advertising that you are eighty—to show what the springs have done for you. It's enough to make a man die of senility to have ten years tacked to his age."

"And if," he went on, "if anything happens to me, Minnie, I'm counting on you to do what you can for the old place. You've been here a good many years, Minnie."

"Fourteen years I have been ladling out water at this spring," I said, trying to keep my lips from trembling. "I wouldn't be at home any place else, unless it would be in an aquarium. But don't ask me to stay here and help Mr. Dick sell the old place for a summer hotel. For that's what he'll do."

"He won't sell it," declared the old doctor grimly. "All I want is for you to promise to stay."

"Oh, I'll stay," I said. "I won't promise to be agreeable, but I'll stay. Somebody'll have to look after the spring; I reckon Mr. Dick thinks it comes out of the earth just as we sell it, with the whole pharmacopoeia in it."

Well, it made the old doctor happier, and I'm not sorry I promised, but I've got a joint on my right foot that throbs when it is going to rain or I am going to have bad luck, and it gave a jump then. I might have known there was trouble ahead.

CHAPTER II

MISS PATTY ARRIVES

It was pretty quiet in the spring-house that day after the old doctor left. It had started to snow and only the regulars came out. What with the old doctor talking about dying, and Miss Patty Jennings gone to Mexico, when I'd been looking forward to her and her cantankerous old father coming to Hope Springs for February, as they mostly did, I was depressed all day. I got to the point where Mr. Moody feeding nickels into the slot-machine with one hand and eating zwieback with the other made me nervous. After a while he went to sleep over it, and when he had slipped a nickel in his mouth and tried to put the zwieback in the machine he muttered something and went up to the house.

I was glad to be alone. I drew a chair in front of the fire and wondered what I would do if the old doctor died, and what a fool I'd been not to be a school-teacher, which is what I studied for.

I was thinking to myself bitterly that all that my experience in the spring fitted me for was to be a mermaid, when I heard something running down the path, and it turned out to be Tillie, the diet cook.

She slammed the door behind her and threw the Finleyville evening paper at me.

"There!" she said, "I've won a cake of toilet soap from Bath-house Mike. The emperor's consented."

"Nonsense!" I snapped, and snatched the paper. Tillie was right; the emperor HAD! I sat down and read it through, and there was Miss Patty's picture in an oval and the prince's in another, with a turned-up mustache and his hand on the handle of his sword, and between them both was the Austrian emperor. Tillie came and looked over my shoulder.

"I'm not keen on the mustache," she said, "but the sword's beautiful—and, oh, Minnie, isn't he aristocratic? Look at his nose!"

But I'm not one to make up my mind in a hurry, and I'd heard enough talk about foreign marriages in the years I'd been dipping out mineral water to make me a skeptic, so to speak.

"I'm not so sure," I said slowly. "You can't tell anything by that kind of a picture. If he was even standing beside a chair I could get a line on him. He may be only four feet high."

"Then Miss Jennings wouldn't love him," declared Tillie. "How do you reckon he makes his mustache point up like that?"

"What's love got to do with it?" I demanded. "Don't be a fool, Tillie. It takes more than two people's pictures in a newspaper with a red heart around them and an overweight cupid above to make a love-match. Love's a word that's used to cover a good many sins and to excuse them all."

"She isn't that kind," said Tillie. "She's—she's as sweet as she's beautiful, and you're as excited as I am, Minnie Waters, and if you're not, what have you got the drinking glass she used last winter put on the top shelf out of reach for?" She went to the door and slammed it open. "Thank heaven I'm not a dried-up old maid," she called back over her shoulder, "and when you're through hugging that paper you can send it up to the house."

Well, I sat there and thought it over, Miss Patty, or Miss Patricia, being, so to speak, a friend of mine. They'd come to the Springs every winter for years. Many a time she'd slipped away from her governess and come down to the spring-house for a chat with me, and we'd make pop-corn together by my open fire, and talk about love and clothes, and even the tariff, Miss Patty being for protection, which was natural, seeing that was the way her father made his money, and I for free trade, especially in the winter when my tips fall off considerable.

And when she was younger she would sit back from the fire, with the corn-popper on her lap and her cheeks as red as cranberries, and say: "I DON'T know why I tell you all these things, Minnie, but

Aunt Honoria's funny, and I can't talk to Dorothy; she's too young, you know. Well, HE said—" only every winter it was a different "he."

In my wash-stand drawer I'd kept all the clippings about her coming out and the winter she spent in Washington and was supposed to be engaged to the president's son, and the magazine article that told how Mr. Jennings had got his money by robbing widows and orphans, and showed the little frame house where Miss Patty was born—as if she's had anything to do with it. And so now I was cutting out the picture of her and the prince and the article underneath which told how many castles she'd have, and I don't mind saying I was sniffling a little bit, for I couldn't get used to the idea. And suddenly the door closed softly and there was a rustle behind me. When I turned it was Miss Patty herself. She saw the clipping immediately, and stopped just inside the door.

"YOU, TOO," she said. "And we've come all this distance to get away from just that."

"Well, I shan't talk about it," I replied, not holding out my hand, for with her, so to speak, next door to being a princess—but she leaned right over and kissed me. I could hardly believe it.

"Why won't you talk about it?" she insisted, catching me by the shoulders and holding me off. "Minnie, your eyes are as red as your hair!"

"I don't approve of it," I said. "You might as well know it now as later, Miss Patty. I don't believe in mixed marriages. I had a cousin that married a Jew, and what with him making the children promise to be good on the Talmud and her trying to raise them with the Bible, the poor things is that mixed up that it's pitiful."

She got a little red at that, but she sat down and took up the clipping.

"He's much better looking than that, Minnie," she said soberly, "and he's a good Catholic. But if that's the way you feel we'll not talk about it. I've had enough trouble at home as it is."

"I guess from that your father isn't crazy about it," I remarked, getting her a glass of spring water. The papers had been full of how Mr. Jennings had forbidden the prince the house when he had been in America the summer before.

"Certainly he's crazy about it—almost insane!" she said, and smiled at me in her old way over the top of the glass. Then she put down the glass and came over to me. "Minnie, Minnie," she said, "if you only knew how I've wanted to get away from the newspapers and the gossips and come to this smelly little spring-house and talk things over with a red-haired, sharp-tongued, mean-dispositioned spring-house girl—!"

And with that I began to blubber, and she came into my arms like a baby.

"You're all I've got," I declared, over and over, "and you're going to live in a country where they harness women with dogs, and you'll never hear an English word from morning to night."

"Stuff!" She gave me a little shake. "He speaks as good English as I do. And now we're going to stop talking about him—you're worse than the newspapers." She took off her things and going into my closet began to rummage for the pop-corn. "Oh, how glad I am to get away," she sang out to me. "We're supposed to have gone to Mexico; even Dorothy doesn't know. Where's the pop-corner or the corn-popper or whatever you call it?"

She was as happy to have escaped the reporters and the people she knew as a child, and she sat down on the floor in front of the fire and began to shell the corn into the popper, as if she'd done it only the day before.

"I guess you're safe enough here," I said. "It's always slack in January—only a few chronics and the Saturday-to-Monday husbands, except a drummer now and then who drives up from Finleyville. It's too early for drooping society buds, and the chronic livers don't get around until late March, after the banquet season closes. It will be pretty quiet for a while."

And at that minute the door was flung open, and Bath-house Mike staggered in.

"The old doctor!" he gasped. "He's dead, Miss Minnie—died just now in the hot room in the bathhouse! One minute he was givin' me the divil for something or other, and the next—I thought he was asleep."

Something that had been heavy in my breast all afternoon suddenly seemed to burst and made me feel faint all over. But I didn't lose my head.

"Does anybody know yet?" I asked quickly. He shook his head.

"Then he didn't die in the bath-house, Mike," I said firmly. "He died in his bed, and you know it. If it gets out that he died in the hot room I'll have the coroner on you."

Miss Patty was standing by the railing of the spring. I got my shawl and started out after Mike, and she followed.

"If the guests ever get hold of this they'll stampede. Start any excitement in a sanatorium," I said, "and one and all they'll dip their thermometers in hot water and swear they've got fever!"

And we hurried to the house together.

CHAPTER III

A WILL

Well, we got the poor old doctor moved back to his room, and had one of the chambermaids find him there, and I wired to Mrs. Van Alstyne, who was Mr. Dicky Carter's sister, and who was on her honeymoon in South Carolina. The Van Alstynes came back at once, in very bad tempers, and we had the funeral from the preacher's house in Finleyville so as not to harrow up the sanatorium people any more than necessary. Even as it was a few left, but about twenty of the chronics stayed, and it looked as if we might be able to keep going.

Miss Patty sent to town for a black veil for me, and even went to the funeral. It helped to take my mind off my troubles to think who it was that was holding my hand and comforting me, and when, toward the end of the service, she got out her handkerchief and wiped her eyes I was almost overcome, she being, so to speak, in the very shadow of a throne.

After it was all over the relatives gathered in the sun parlor of the sanatorium to hear the will—Mr. Van Alstyne and his wife and about twenty more who had come up from the city for the funeral and stayed over—on the house.

Well, the old doctor left me the buttons for his full dress waistcoat and his favorite copy of Gray's Anatomy. I couldn't exactly set up housekeeping with my share of the estate, but when the lawyer read that part of the will aloud and a grin went around the room I flounced out of my chair.

"Maybe you think I'm disappointed," I said, looking hard at the family, who weren't making any particular pretense at grief, and at the house people standing around the door. "Maybe you think it's funny to see an unmarried woman get a set of waistcoat buttons and a medical book. Well, that set of buttons was the set he bought in London on his wedding trip, and the book's the one he read himself to sleep with every night for twenty years. I'm proud to get them."

Mr. Van Alstyne touched me on the arm.

"Everybody knows how loyal you've been, Minnie," he assured me. "Now sit down like a good girl and listen to the rest of the will."

"While I'm up I might as well get something else off my mind," I said. "I know what's in that will, but I hadn't anything to do with it, Mr. Van Alstyne. He took advantage of my being laid up with influenza last spring."

They thought that was funny, but a few minutes later they weren't so cheerful. You see the sanatorium was a mighty fine piece of property, with a deer park and golf links. We'd had plenty of offers to sell it for a summer hotel, but we'd both been dead against it. That was one of the reasons for the will.

The whole estate was left to Dicky Carter, who hadn't been able to come, owing to his being laid up with an attack of mumps. The family sat up and nodded at one another, or held up its hands, but when they heard there was a condition they breathed easier.

Beginning with one week after the reading of the will—and not a day later—Mr. Dick was to take charge of the sanatorium and to stay there for two months without a day off. If at the end of that time the place was being successfully conducted and could show that it hadn't lost money, the entire property became his for keeps. If he failed it was to be sold and the money given to charity.

You would have to know Richard Carter to understand the excitement the will caused. Most of us, I reckon, like the sort of person we've never dared to be ourselves. The old doctor had gone to bed at ten o'clock all his life and got up at seven, and so he had a sneaking fondness for the one particular grandson who often didn't go to bed at all. Twice to my knowledge when he was in his teens did Dicky Carter run away from school, and twice his grandfather kept him for a week hidden in the shelter-house on the golf links. Naturally when Mr. Van Alstyne and I had to hide him again, which is further on in the story, he went to the old shelter-house like a dog to its kennel, only this time—but that's ahead, too.

Well, the family went back to town in a buzz of indignation, and I carried my waistcoat buttons and my Anatomy out to the spring-house and had a good cry. There was a man named Thoburn who was crazy for the property as a summer hotel, and every time I shut my eyes I could see "Thoburn House" over the veranda and children sailing paper boats in the mineral spring.

Sure enough, the next afternoon Mr. Thoburn drove out from Finleyville with a suit case, and before he'd taken off his overcoat he came out to the spring-house.

"Hello, Minnie," he exclaimed. "Does the old man's ghost come back to dope the spring, or do you do it?"

"I don't know what you are talking about, Mr. Thoburn," I retorted sharply. "If you don't know that this spring has its origin in—"

"In Schmidt's drug store down in Finleyville!" he finished for me. "Oh, I know all about that spring, Minnie! Don't forget that my father's cows used to drink that water and liked it. I leave it to you," he said, sniffing, "if a self-respecting cow wouldn't die of thirst before she drank that stuff as it is now."

I'd been filling him a glass—it being a matter of habit with me—and he took it to the window and held it to the light.

"You're getting careless, Minnie," he said, squinting at it. "Some of those drugs ought to be dissolved first in hot water. There's a lump of lithia there that has Schmidt's pharmacy label on it."

"Where?" I demanded, and started for it. He laughed at that, and putting the glass down, he came over and stood smiling at me.

"As ingenuous as a child," he said in his mocking way, "a nice, little red-haired child! Minnie, how old is this young Carter?"

"Twenty-three."

"An—er—earnest youth? Willing to buckle down to work and make the old place go? Ready to pat the old ladies on the shoulder and squeeze the young ones' hands?"

"He's young," I said, "but if you're counting on his being a fool—"

"Not at all," he broke in hastily. "If he hasn't too much character he'll probably succeed. I hope he isn't a fool. If he isn't, oh, friend Minnie, he'll stand the atmosphere of this Garden of Souls for about a week, and then he'll kill some of them and escape. Where is he now?"

"He's been sick," I said. "Mumps!"

"Mumps! Oh, my aunt!" he exclaimed, and fell to laughing. He was still laughing when he got to the door.

"Mumps!" he repeated, with his hand on the knob. "Minnie, the old place will be under the hammer in three weeks, and if you know what's good for you, you'll sign in under the new management while there's a vacancy. You've been the whole show here for so long that it will be hard for you to line up in the back row of the chorus."

"If I were you," I said, looking him straight in the eye, "I wouldn't pick out any new carpets yet, Mr. Thoburn. I promised the old doctor I'd help Mr. Dick, and I will."

"So you're actually going to fight it out," he said, grinning. "Well, the odds are in your favor. You are two to my one."

"I think it's pretty even," I retorted. "We will be hindered, so to speak, by having certain principles of honor and honesty. You have no handicap."

He tried to think of a retort, and not finding one he slammed out of the spring-house in a rage.

Mr. Van Alstyne and his wife came in that same day, just before dinner, and we played three-handed bridge for half an hour. As I've said, they'd been on their honeymoon, and they were both sulky at having to stay at the Springs. It was particularly hard on Mrs. Van Alstyne, because, with seven trunks of trousseau with her, she had to put on black. But she used to shut herself up in her room in the evenings and deck out for Mr. Sam in her best things. We found it out one evening when Mrs. Biggs set fire to her bureau cover with her alcohol curling-iron heater, and Mrs. Sam, who had been going around in a black crepe dress all day, rushed out in pink satin with crystal trimming, and slippers with cut-glass heels.

After the first rubber Mrs. Van Alstyne threw her cards on the floor and said another day like this would finish her.

"Surely Dick is able to come now," she said, like a peevish child. "Didn't he say the swelling was all gone?"

"Do you expect me to pick up those cards?" Mr. Sam asked angrily, looking at her.

Mrs. Sam yawned and looked up at him.

"Of course I do," she answered. "If it wasn't for you I'd not have stayed a moment after the funeral. Isn't it bad enough to have seven trunks full of clothes I've never worn, and to have to put on poky old black, without keeping me here in this old ladies' home?"

Mr. Sam looked at the cards and then at her.

"I'm not going to pick them up," he declared. "And as to our staying here, don't you realize that if we don't your precious brother will never show up here at all, or stay if he does come? And don't you also realize that this is probably the only chance he'll ever have in the world to become financially independent of us?"

"You needn't be brutal," she said sharply. "And it isn't so bad for you here as it is for me. You spend every waking minute admiring Miss Jennings, while I—there isn't a man in the place who'll talk anything but his joints or his stomach."

She got up and went to the window, and Mr. Sam followed her. Nobody pays any attention to me in the spring-house; I'm a part of it, like the brass rail around the spring, or the clock.

"I'm not admiring Miss Jennings," he corrected, "I'm sympathizing, dear. She looks too nice a girl to have been stung by the title bee, that's all."

She turned her back to him, but he pretended to tuck the hair at the back of her neck up under her comb, and she let him do it. As I stooped to gather up the cards he kissed the tip of her ear.

"Listen," he said, "there's a scream of a play down at Finleyville to-night called Sweet Peas. Senator Biggs and the bishop went down last night, and they say it's the worst in twenty years. Put on a black veil and let's slip away and see it."

I think she agreed to do it, but that night after dinner, Amanda King, who has charge of the news stand, told me the sheriff had closed the opera-house and that the leading woman was sick at the hotel.

"They say she looked funny last night," Amanda finished, "and I guess she's got the mumps."

Mumps!

My joint gave a throb at that minute.

CHAPTER IV

AND A WAY

Mr. Sam wasn't taking any chances, for the next day he went to the city himself to bring Mr. Dick up. Everything was quiet that day and the day after, except that on the second day I had a difference of opinion with the house doctor and he left.

The story of the will had got out, of course, and the guests were waiting to see Mr. Dick come and take charge. I got a good bit of gossip from Miss Cobb, who had had her hair cut short after a fever and used to come out early in the morning and curl it all over her head, heating the curler on the fire log. I never smell burnt hair that I don't think of Miss Cobb trying to do the back of her neck. She was one of our regulars, and every winter for ten years she'd read me the letters she had got from an insurance agent who'd run away with a married woman the day before the wedding. She kept them in a bundle, tied with lavender ribbon.

It was on the third day, I think, that Miss Cobb told me that Miss Patty and her father had had a quarrel the day before. She got it from one of the chambermaids. Mr. Jennings was a liver case and not pleasant at any time, but he had been worse than usual. Annie, the chambermaid, told Miss Cobb that the trouble was about settlements, and that the more Miss Patty tried to tell him it was the European custom the worse he got. Miss Patty hadn't come down to breakfast that day, and Mr. Moody and Senator Biggs made a wager in the Turkish bath—according to Miss Cobb—Mr. Moody betting the wedding wouldn't come off at all.

"Of course," Miss Cobb said, wetting her finger and trying the iron to see if it was hot, "of course, Minnie, they're not married yet, and if Father Jennings gets ugly and makes any sort of scandal it's all off. A scandal just now would be fatal. These royalties are very touchy about other people's reputations."

Well, I heard that often enough in the next few days.

Mr. Sam hadn't come back by the morning of the sixth day, but he wired his wife the day before that Mr. Dick was on the way. But we met every train with a sleigh, and he didn't come. I was uneasy, knowing Mr. Dick, and Mrs. Sam was worried, too.

By that time everybody was waiting and watching, and on the early train on the sixth day came the lawyer, a Mr. Stitt. Mr. Thoburn was going around with a sort of greasy smile, and if I could have poisoned him safely I'd have done it.

It had been snowing hard for a day or so, and at eleven o'clock that day I saw Miss Cobb and Mrs. Biggs coming down the path to the spring-house, Mrs. Biggs with her crocheting-bag hanging to the handle of her umbrella. I opened the door, but they wouldn't come in.

"We won't track up your clean floor, Minnie," Mrs. Biggs said—she was a little woman, almost fifty, who'd gone through life convinced she'd only lived so long by the care she took of herself—"but I thought I'd better come and speak to you. Please don't irritate Mr. Biggs to-day. He's been reading that article of Upton Sinclair's about fasting, and hasn't had a bite to eat since noon yesterday."

I noticed then that she looked pale. She was a nervous creature, although she could drink more spring water than any human being I ever saw, except one man, and he was a German.

Well, I promised to be careful. I've seen them fast before, and when a fat man starts to live on his own fat, like a bear, he gets about the same disposition.

Mrs. Biggs started back, but Miss Cobb waited a moment at the foot of the steps.

"Mr. Van Alstyne is back," she said, "but he came alone."

"Alone!" I repeated, staring at her in a sort of daze.

"Alone," she said solemnly, "and I heard him ask for Mr. Carter. It seems he started for here yesterday."

But I'd had time to get myself in hand, and if I had a chill up my spine she never knew it. As she started after Mrs. Biggs I saw Mr. Sam hurrying down the path toward the spring-house, and I knew my joint hadn't throbbed for nothing.

Mr. Sam came in and slammed the door behind him.

"What's this about Mr. Dick not being here?" he shouted.

"Well, he isn't. That's all there is to it, Mr. Van Alstyne," I said calmly. I am always calm when other people get excited. For that reason some people think my red hair is a false alarm, but they soon find out.

"But he MUST be here," said Mr. Van Alstyne. "I put him on the train myself yesterday, and waited until it started to be sure he was off."

"The only way to get Mr. Richard anywhere you want him to go," I said dryly, "is to have him nailed in a crate and labeled."

"Damned young scamp!" said Mr. Van Alstyne, although I have a sign in the spring-house, "Profanity not allowed."

"EXACTLY what was he doing when you last laid eyes on him?" I asked.

"He was on the train—"

"Was he alone?"

"Yes."

"Sitting?"

"No, standing. What the deuce, Minnie—"

"Waving out the window to you?"

"Of course not!" exclaimed Mr. Van Alstyne testily. "He was raising the window for a girl in the next seat."

"Precisely!" I said. "Would you know the girl well enough to trace her?"

"That's ridiculous, you know," he said trying to be polite. "Out of a thousand and one things that may have detained him—"

"Only one thing ever detains Mr. Dick, and that always detains him," I said solemnly. "That's a girl. You're a newcomer in the family, Mr. Van Alstyne; you don't remember the time he went down here to the station to see his Aunt Agnes off to the city, and we found him three weeks later in Oklahoma trying to marry a widow with five children."

Mr. Van Alstyne dropped into a chair, and through force of habit I gave him a glass of spring water.

"This was a pretty girl, too," he said dismally.

I sat down on the other side of the fireplace, and it seemed to me that father's crayon enlargement over the mantel shook its head at me.

After a minute Mr. Van Alstyne drank the water and got up.

"I'll have to tell my wife," he said. "Who's running the place, anyhow? You?"

"Not—exactly," I explained, "but, of course, when anything comes up they consult me. The housekeeper is a fool, and now that the house doctor's gone—"

"Gone! Who's looking after the patients?"

"Well, most of them have been here before," I explained, "and I know their treatment—the kind of baths and all that."

"Oh, YOU know the treatment!" he said, eying me. "And why did the house doctor go?"

"He ordered Mr. Moody to take his spring water hot. Mr. Moody's spring water has been ordered cold for eleven years, and I refused to change. It was between the doctor and me, Mr. Van Alstyne."

"Oh, of course," he said, "if it was a matter of principle—" He stopped, and then something seemed to strike him. "I say," he said; "about the doctor—that's all right, you know; lots of doctors and all that. But for heaven's sake, Minnie, don't discharge the cook."

Now that was queer, for it had been running in my head all morning that in the slack season it would be cheaper to get a good woman instead of the chef and let Tillie, the diet cook, make the pastry.

Mr. Sam picked up his hat and looked at his watch.

"Eleven thirty," he said, "and no sign of that puppy yet. I guess it's up to the police."

"If there was only something to do," I said, with a lump in my throat, "but to have to sit and do nothing while the old place dies it's—it's awful, Mr. Van Alstyne."

"We're not dead yet," he replied from the door, "and maybe we'll need you before the day's over. If anybody can sail the old bark to shore, you can do it, Minnie. You've been steering it for years. The old doctor was no navigator, and you and I know it."

It was blowing a blizzard by that time, and Miss Patty was the only one who came out to the spring-house until after three o'clock. She shook the snow off her furs and stood by the fire, looking at me and not saying anything for fully a minute.

"Well," she said finally, "aren't you ashamed of yourself?"

"Why?" I asked, and swallowed hard.

"To be in all this trouble and not let me know. I've just this minute heard about it. Can't we get the police?"

"Mr. Van Alstyne is trying," I said, "but I don't hope much. Like as not Mr. Dick will turn up tomorrow and say his calendar was a day slow."

I gave her a glass of water, and I noticed when she took it how pale she was. But she held it up and smiled over it at me.

"Here's to everything turning out better than we expect!" she said, and made a face as she drank the water. I thought that she was thinking of her own troubles as well as mine, for she put down the glass and stood looking at her engagement ring, a square red ruby in an old-fashioned setting. It was a very large ruby, but I've seen showier rings.

"There isn't anything wrong, Miss Patty, is there?" I asked, and she dropped her hand and looked at me.

"Oh, no," she said. "That is, nothing much, Minnie. Father is—I think he's rather ridiculous about some things, but I dare say he'll come around. I don't mind his fussing with me, but—if it should get in the papers, Minnie! A breath of unpleasant notoriety now would be fatal!"

"I don't see why," I said sharply. "The royal families of Europe have a good bit of unpleasant notoriety themselves occasionally. I should think they'd fall over themselves to get some good red American blood. Blue blood's bad blood; you can ask any doctor."

But she only smiled.

"You're like father, Minnie," she said. "You'll never understand."

"I'm not sure I want to," I snapped, and fell to polishing glasses.

The storm stopped a little at three and most of the guests waded down through the snow for bridge and spring water. By that time the afternoon train was in, and no Mr. Dick. Mr. Sam was keeping the lawyer, Mr. Stitt, in the billiard room, and by four o'clock they'd had everything that was in the bar and were inventing new combinations of their own. And Mrs. Sam had gone to bed with a nervous headache.

Senator Biggs brought the mail down to the spring-house at four, but there was nothing for me except a note from Mr. Sam, rather shaky, which said he'd no word yet and that Mr. Stitt had mixed all the cordials in the bar in a beer glass and had had to go to bed.

At half past four Mr. Thoburn came out for a minute. He said there was only one other train from town that night and the chances were it would be snowed up at the junction.

"Better get on the band wagon before the parade's gone past," he said in an undertone. But I went into my pantry and shut the door with a slam, and when I came out he was gone.

I nearly went crazy that afternoon. I put salt in Miss Cobb's glass when she always drank the water plain. Once I put the broom in the fire and started to sweep the porch with a fire log Luckily they were busy with their letters and it went unnoticed, the smell of burning straw not rising, so to speak, above the sulphur in the spring.

Senator Biggs went from one table to another telling how well he felt since he stopped eating, and trying to coax the other men to starve with him.

It's funny how a man with a theory about his stomach isn't happy until he has made some other fellow swallow it.

"Well," he said, standing in front of the fire with a glass of water in his hand, "it's worth while to feel like this. My head's as clear as a bell. I don't care to eat; I don't want to eat. The 'fast' is the solution."

"Two stages to that solution, Senator," said the bishop; "first, resolution; last, dissolution."

Then they all began at once. If you have ever heard twenty people airing their theories on diet you know all about it. One shouts for Horace Fletcher, and another one swears by the scraped-beef treatment, and somebody else never touches a thing but raw eggs and milk, and pretty soon there is a riot of calories and carbohydrates. It always ends the same way: the man with the loudest voice wins, and the defeated ones limp over to the spring and tell their theories to me. They know I'm being paid to listen.

On this particular afternoon the bishop stopped the riot by rising and holding up his hand. "Ladies and gentlemen," he said, "let us not be rancorous. If each of us has a theory, and that theory works out to his satisfaction, then—why are we all here?"

"Merely to tell one another the good news!" Mr. Jennings said sourly from his corner.

Honest, it was funny. If some folks were healthy they'd be lonesome.

But when things had got quiet—except Mr. Moody dropping nickels into the slot-machine—I happened to look over at Miss Patty, and I saw there was something wrong. She had a letter open in her lap not one of the blue ones with the black and gold seal that every one in the house knew came from the prince but a white one, and she was staring at it as if she'd seen a ghost.

CHAPTER V

WANTED—AN OWNER

I have never reproached Miss Patty, but if she had only given me the letter to read or had told me the whole truth instead of a part of it, I would have understood, and things would all have been different. It is all very well for her to say that I looked worried enough already, and that anyhow it was a family affair. I SHOULD HAVE BEEN TOLD.

All she did was to come up to me as I stood in the spring, with her face perfectly white, and ask me if my Dicky Carter was the Richard Carter who stayed at the Grosvenor in town.

"He doesn't stay anywhere," I said, with my feet getting cold, "but that's where he has apartments. What has he been doing now?"

"You're expecting him on the evening train, aren't you?" she asked. "Don't stare like that: my father's watching."

"He ought to be on the evening train," I said. I wasn't going to say I expected him. I didn't.

"Listen, Minnie," she said, "you'll have to send him away again the moment he comes. He must not go into the house."

I stood looking at her, with my mouth open.

"Not go into the house," I repeated, "with everybody waiting for him for the last six days, and Mr. Stitt here to turn things over to him!"

She stood tapping her foot, with her pretty brows knitted.

"The wretch!" she cried, "the hateful creature as if things weren't bad enough! I suppose he'll have to come, Minnie, but I must see him before he sees any one else."

Just then the bishop brought his glass over to the spring.

"Hot this time, Minnie," he said. "Do you know, I'm getting the mineral-water habit, Patty! I'm afraid plain water will have no attraction for me after this."

He put his hand over hers on the rail. They were old friends, the bishop and the Jenningses.

"Well, how goes it to-day with the father?" he said in a low tone, and smiling.

Miss Patty shrugged her shoulders. "Worse, if possible."

"I thought so," he said cheerfully. "If state of mind is any criterion I should think he has had a relapse. A little salt, Minnie." Miss Patty stood watching him while he tasted it.

"Bishop," she said suddenly, "will you do something for me?"

"I always have, Patty." He was very fond of Miss Patty, was the bishop.

"Then—to-night, not later than eight o'clock, get father to play cribbage, will you? And keep him in the card-room until nine."

"Another escapade!" he said, pretending to be very serious. "Patty, Patty, you'll be the death of me yet. Is thy servant a dog, that he should do this thing?"

"Certainly NOT," said Miss Patty. "Just a dear, slightly bald, but still very distinguished slave!"

The bishop picked up her left hand and looked at the ring and from that to her face.

"There will be plenty of slaves to kiss this little hand, where you are going, my child," he said. "Sometimes I wish that some nice red-blooded boy here at home—but I dare say it will turn out surprisingly well as it is."

"Bishop, Bishop!" Mrs. Moody called. "How naughty of you, and with your bridge hand waiting to be held!"

He carried his glass back to the table, stopping for a moment beside Mr. Jennings.

"If Patty becomes any more beautiful," he said, "I shall be in favor of having her wear a mask. How are we young men to protect ourselves?"

"Pretty is as pretty does!" declared Mr. Jennings from behind his newspaper, and Miss Patty went out with her chin up.

Well, I knew Mr. Dick had been up to some mischief; I had suspected it all along. But Miss Patty went to bed, and old Mrs. Hutchins, who's a sort of lady's-maid-companion of hers, said she mustn't be disturbed. I was pretty nearly sick myself. And when Mr. Sam came out at five o'clock and said he'd been in the long-distance telephone booth for an hour and had called everybody who had ever known Mr. Dick, and that he had dropped right off the earth, I just about gave up. He had got some detectives, he said, and there was some sort of a story about his having kept right on the train to Salem, Ohio, but if he had they'd lost the trail there, and anyhow, with the railroad service tied up by the storm there wasn't much chance of his getting to Finleyville in time.

Luckily Mr. Stitt was in bed with a mustard leaf over his stomach and ice on his head, and didn't know whether it was night or morning. But Thoburn was going around with a watch in his hand, and Mr. Sam was for killing him and burying the body in the snow.

At half past five I just about gave up. I was sitting in front of the fire wondering why I'd taken influenza the spring before from getting my feet wet in a shower, when I had been standing in a mineral spring for so many years that it's a wonder I'm not web-footed. It was when I had influenza that the old doctor made the will, you remember. Maybe I was crying, I don't recall.

It was dark outside, and nothing inside but firelight. Suddenly I seemed to feel somebody looking at the back of my neck and I turned around. There was a man standing outside one of the windows, staring in.

My first thought, of course, was that it was Mr. Dick, but just as the face vanished I saw that it wasn't. It was older by three or four years than Mr. Dick's and a bit fuller.

I'm not nervous. I've had to hold my own against chronic grouches too long to have nerves, so I went to the door and looked out. The man came around the corner just then and I could see him plainly in the firelight. He was covered with snow, and he wore a sweater and no overcoat, but he looked like a gentleman.

"I beg your pardon for spying," he said, "but the fire looked so snug! I've been trying to get to the hotel over there, but in the dark I've lost the path."

"That's not a hotel," I snapped, for that touched me on the raw. "That's Hope Springs Sanatorium, and this is one of the Springs."

"Oh, Hope Springs, internal instead of eternal!" he said. "That's awfully bad, isn't it? To tell you the truth, I think I'd better come in and get some; I'm short on hope just now."

I thought that was likely enough, for although his voice was cheerful and his eyes smiled, there was a drawn look around his mouth, and he hadn't shaved that day. I wish I had had as much experience in learning what's right with folks as I have had in learning what's wrong with them.

"You'd better come in and get warm, anyhow," I told him, "only don't spring any more gags. I've been 'Hebe' for fourteen years and I've served all the fancy drinks you can name over the brass railing of that spring. Nowadays, when a fellow gets smart and asks for a Mamie Taylor, I charge him a Mamie Taylor price."

He shut the door behind him and came over to the fire.

"I'm pretty well frozen," he said. "Don't be astonished if I melt before your eyes; I've been walking for hours."

Now that I had a better chance to see him I'd sized up that drawn look around his mouth.

"Missed your luncheon, I suppose," I said, poking the fire log. He grinned rather sheepishly.

"Well, I haven't had any, and I've certainly missed it," he said.

"Fasting's healthy, you know."

I thought of Senator Biggs, who carried enough fat to nourish him for months, and then I looked at my visitor, who hadn't an ounce of extra flesh on him.

"Nothing's healthy that isn't natural," I declared. "If you'd care for a dish of buttered and salted pop-corn, there's some on the mantel. It's pretty salty; the idea is to make folks thirsty so they'll enjoy the mineral water."

"Think of raising a real thirst only to drown it with spring water!" he said. But he got the pop corn and he ate it all. If he hadn't had any luncheon he hadn't had much breakfast. The queer part was—he was a gentleman; his clothes were the right sort, but he had on patent leather shoes in all that snow and an automobile cap.

I put away the glasses while he ate. Pretty soon he looked up and the drawn lines were gone. He wasn't like Mr. Dick, but he was the same type, only taller and heavier built.

"And so it isn't a hotel," he remarked. "Well, I'm sorry. The caravansary in the village is not to my liking, and I had thought of engaging a suite up here. My secretary usually attends to these things, but—don't take away all the glasses, Heb—I beg your pardon—but the thirst is coming."

He filled the glass himself and then he came up and stood in front of me, with the glass held up in the air.

"To the best woman I have met in many days," he said, not mocking but serious. "I was about to lie down and let the little birds cover me with leaves." Then he glanced at the empty dish and smiled. "To buttered pop-corn! Long may it wave!" he said, and emptied the glass.

Well, I found a couple of apples in my pantry and brought them out, and after he ate them he told me what had happened to him. He had been a little of everything since he left college he was about twenty-five had crossed the Atlantic in a catboat and gone with somebody or other into some part of Africa—they got lost and had to eat each other or lizards, or something like that—and then he went to the Philippines, and got stuck there and had to sell books to get home. He had a little money, "enough for a grub-stake," he said, and all his folks were dead. Then a college friend of his wrote a rural play called Sweet Peas—"Great title, don't you think?" he asked—and he put up all the money. It would have been a hit, he said, but the kid in the play—the one that unites its parents in the last act just before he dies of tuberculosis—the kid took the mumps and looked as if, instead of fading away, he was going to blow up. Everybody was so afraid of him that they let him die alone for three nights in the middle of the stage. Then the leading woman took the mumps, and the sheriff took everything else.

"You city folks seem to know so much," I said, "and yet you bring a country play to the country! Why don't you bring out a play with women in low-necked gowns, and champagne suppers, and a scandal or two? They packed Pike's Opera-House three years ago with a play called Why Women Sin."

Well, of course, the thing failed, and he lost every dollar he'd put into it, which was all he had, including what he had in his pockets.

"They seized my trunks," he explained, "and I sold my fur-lined overcoat for eight dollars, which took one of the girls back home. It's hard for the women. A fellow can always get some sort of a job—I was coming up here to see if they needed an extra clerk or a waiter, or chauffeur, or anything that meant a roof and something to eat—but I suppose they don't need a jack-of-all-trades."

"No," I answered, "but I'll tell you what I think they're going to need. And that's an owner!"

CHAPTER VI

THE CONSPIRACY

I'm not making any excuses. I did it for the best. In any sort of crisis there are always folks who stand around and wring their hands and say, "What shall we do?" And then if it's a fire and somebody has had enough sense to send for the engines, they say: "Just look at what the water did!" Although as far as I can see I'm the only one that suffered any damage.

If Mr. Thoburn had not been there, sitting by to see the old sanatorium die so it could sprout wings and fly as a summer hotel, I'd never have thought of it. But I was in despair.

I got up and opened the door, but the Snow came in in a cloud, and the path was half a foot deep again. It shows on what little threads big things hang, for when I saw the storm I gave up the idea of bringing Mr. Sam down to see the young man, and the breath of fresh air in my face brought me to my senses.

But the angel of providence appeared in the shape of Mike, the bath man, coming down through the snow in a tearing rage. The instant I saw Mike I knew it was settled.

"Am I or am I not to give Mr. Moody a needle shower?" he shouted, almost beside himself. And I saw he had his overcoat over his bath costume, which is a Turkish towel.

"A needle shower followed by a salt rub," said I. "He's been having them for eleven years. What's the matter?"

"That fool of a young doctor," shouted Mike, "he told him before he left that if he'd been taking them for eleven years and wasn't any better it was time to stop. Ain't business bad enough—only four people in the house takin' baths regular—without his buttin' in!"

"Where's Mr. Moody?"

"In the bath. I've locked up his clothes."

"You give him a needle shower and a salt rub," I ordered, "and if he makes a fuss just send for me. And, Mike," I said, as he started out, "ask Mr. Van Alstyne to come out here immediately."

That's the way it was all the time. Everybody brought their troubles to me, and I guess I thought I was a little tin god on wheels and the place couldn't get along without me. But it did; it does. We all think we'll leave a big hole behind us when we go, but it's just like taking your thumb out of a bowl of soup. There isn't even a dent.

Mr. Van Alstyne came out on the run, and when he saw Mr. Pierce by the fire—that was his name, Alan Pierce—he stopped and stared. Then he said:

"You infernal young scamp!" And with that Mr. Pierce jumped up, surprised and pretty mad, and Mr. Van Alstyne saw his mistake.

"I'm sure I beg your pardon!" he said. "The fact is, I was expecting somebody else, and in the firelight—"

"You surprised me, that's all," said Mr. Pierce. "Under the circumstances, I'm glad I'm not the other chap."

"You may be," assured Mr. Sam grimly. "You're not unlike him, by the way. A little taller and heavier, but—"

Now it's all very well for Mr. Sam to say I originated the idea and all that, but as truly as I am writing this, as I watched his face I saw the same thought come into it. He looked Mr. Pierce up and down, and then he stared into the fire and puckered his mouth to whistle, but he didn't. And finally he glanced at me, but I was looking into the fire, too.

"Just come, haven't you?" he asked. "How did you get up the hill?"

"Walked," said Mr. Pierce, smiling. "It took some digging, too. But I didn't come for my health, unless you think three meals a day are necessary for health."

Mr. Sam turned and stared at him. "By Jove! you don't mean it!"

"I wish I didn't," Mr. Pierce replied. "One of the hardest things I've had to remember for the last ten hours was that for two years I voluntarily ate only two meals a day. A man's a fool to do a thing like that! It's reckless."

Mr. Sam got up and began to walk the floor, his hands in his pockets. He tried to get my eye, but still I looked in the fire.

"All traffic's held up, Minnie," he said. "The eight o'clock train is stalled beyond the junction, in a drift. I've wired the conductor, and Carter isn't on it."

"Well?" said I.

"If we could only get past to-day," Mr. Sam went on; "if Thoburn would only choke to death, or—if there was somebody around who looked like Dick. I dare say, by to-morrow—" He looked at Mr. Pierce, who smiled and looked at him.

"And I resemble Dick!" said Mr. Pierce. "Well, if he's a moral and upright young man—"

"He isn't!" Mr. Sam broke in savagely. And then and there he sat down and told Mr. Pierce the trouble we were in, and what sort of cheerful idiot Dicky Carter was, and how everybody liked him, but wished he would grow up before the family good name was gone, and that now he had a chance to make good and be self-supporting, and he wasn't around, and if Mr. Sam ever got his hands on him he'd choke a little sense down his throat.

And then Mr. Pierce told about the play and the mumps, and how he was stranded. When Mr. Sam asked him outright if he'd take Mr. Dick's place overnight he agreed at once.

"I haven't anything to lose," he said, "and anyhow I've been on a diet of Sweet Peas so long that a sanatorium is about what I need."

"It's like this," explained Mr. Sam, "Old Stitt is pretty thoroughly jingled—excuse me, Minnie, but it's the fact. I'll take you to his room, with the lights low, and all you'll need to do is to shake hands with him. He's going on the early train to-morrow. Then you needn't mix around much with the guests until to-morrow, and by that time I hope to have Dick within thrashing distance."

Just as they'd got it arranged that Mr. Pierce was to put on Mr. Sam's overcoat and walk down to the village so that he could come up in a sleigh, as if he had driven over from Yorkton—he was only to walk across the hall in front of the office, with his collar up, just enough to show himself and then go to his room with a chill—just as it was all arranged, Mr. Sam thought of something.

"The house people are waiting for Dick," he said to me, "and about forty women are crocheting in the lobby, so they'll be sure to see him. Won't some of them know it isn't Dick?"

I thought pretty fast.

"He hasn't been around much lately," I said. "Nobody would know except Mrs. Wiggins. She'll never forget him; the last time he was here he put on her false front like a beard and wore it down to dinner."

"Then it's all off," he groaned. "She's got as many eyes as a potato."

"And about as much sense," said I. "Fiddlesticks! She's not so good we can't replace her, and what's the use of swallowing a camel and then sticking at a housekeeper?"

"You can't get her out of the house in an hour," he objected, but in a weak voice.

"I can!" I said firmly.

I did. Inside of an hour she went to the clerk, Mr. Slocum, and handed in her resignation. She was a touchy person, but I did NOT say all that was quoted. I did NOT say the kitchen was filthy; I only said it took away my appetite to look in at the door. But she left, which is the point.

Well, I stood in the doorway and watched them disappear in the darkness, and I felt better than I had all day. It's great to be able to DO something, even if that something is wrong. But as I put on my shawl and turned out the lights, I suddenly remembered. Miss Patty would be waiting in the lobby for Mr. Dick, and she would not be crocheting!

CHAPTER VII.

MR. PIERCE ACQUIRES A WIFE

Whoever has charge of the spring-house at Hope Springs takes the news stand in the evening. That's an old rule. The news stand includes tobacco and a circulating library, and is close to the office, and if I missed any human nature at the spring I got it there. If you can't tell all about a man by the way he asks for mineral water and drinks it, by the time you've supplied his literature and his tobacco and heard him grumbling over his bill at the office, you've got a line on him and a hook in it.

After I ate my supper I relieved Amanda King, who runs the news stand in the daytime, when she isn't laid off with the toothache.

Mr. Sam was right. All the women had on their puffs, and they were sitting in a half-circle on each side of the door. Mrs. Sam was there, looking frightened and anxious, and standing near the card-room door was Miss Patty. She was all in white, with two red spots on her cheeks, and I thought if her prince could have seen her then he would pretty nearly have eaten her up. Mr. Thoburn was there, of course, pretending to read the paper, but every now and then he looked at his watch, and once he got up and paced off the lobby, putting down the length in his note-book. I didn't need a mind-reader to tell me he was figuring the cost of a new hardwood floor and four new rugs.

Mr. Sam came to the news stand, and he was so nervous he could hardly light a cigarette.

"I've had a message from one of the detectives," he said. "They've traced him to Salem, Ohio, but they lost him there. If we can only hold on this evening—! Look at that first-night audience!"

"Mr. Pierce is due in three minutes," I told him. "I hope you told him to kiss his sister."

"Nothing of the sort," he objected. "Why should he kiss her? Mrs. Van Alstyne is afraid of the whole thing: she won't stand for that."

"I guess she could endure it," I remarked dryly.

"It's astonishing how much of that sort of thing a woman can bear."

He looked at me and grinned.

"By gad," he said, "I wouldn't be as sophisticated as you are for a good deal. Isn't that the sleigh?"

Everybody had heard it. The women sat up and craned forward to look at the door: Mrs. Sam was sitting forward clutching the arms of her chair. She was in white, having laid off her black for that evening, with a red rose pinned on her so Mr. Pierce would know her. Miss Patty heard the sleigh-bells also, and she turned and came toward the door. Her mouth was set hard, and she was twisting the ruby ring as she always did when she was nervous. And at the same moment Mr. Sam and I both saw it; she was in white, too, and she had a red rose tucked in her belt!

Mr. Sam muttered something and rushed at her, but he was too late. Just as he got to her the door opened and in came Mr. Pierce, with Mr. Sam's fur coat turned up around his ears and Mr. Sam's fur cap drawn well down on his head. He stood for an instant blinking in the light, and Mrs. Van Alstyne got up nervously. He never even saw her. His eyes lighted on Miss Patty's face and stayed there. Mr. Sam was there, but what could he do? Mr. Pierce walked over to Miss Patty, took her hand, said, "Hello there!" and KISSED HER. It was awful.

Most women will do anything to save a scene, and that helped us, for she never turned a hair. But when Mr. Sam got him by the arm and led him toward the stairs, she turned so that the old cats sitting around could not see her and her face was scarlet. She went over to the wood fire—our lobby is a sort of big room with chairs and tables and palms, and an open fire in winter—and sat down. I don't think she knew herself whether she was most astonished or angry.

Mrs. Biggs gave a nasty little laugh.

"Your brother didn't see you," she said to Mrs. Van Alstyne. "I dare say a sister doesn't count much when a future princess is around!"

Mrs. Van Alstyne was still staring up the staircase, but she came to herself at that. She had some grit in her, if she did look like a French doll.

"My brother and Miss Jennings are very old friends," she remarked quietly. I believe that was what she thought, too. I don't think she had seen the other red rose, and what was she to think but that Mr. Pierce had known Miss Jennings somewhere? She was dazed, Mrs. Sam was. But she carried off the situation anyhow, and gave us time to breathe. We needed it.

"If I were his highness," said Miss Cobb, spreading the Irish lace collar she was making over her knee and squinting at it, "I should wish my fiancee to be more er—dignified. Those old Austrian families are very haughty. They would not understand our American habit of osculation."

I was pretty mad at that, for anybody could have seen Miss Patty didn't kiss him.

"If by osculation you mean kissing, Miss Cobb," I said, going over to her, "I guess you don't remember the Austrian count who was a head waiter here. If there was anything in the way of osculation that that member of an old Austrian family didn't know, I've got to find it out. He could kiss all around any American I ever saw!"

I went back to my news stand. I was shaking so my knees would hardly hold me. All I could think of was that they had swallowed Mr. Pierce, bait and hook, and that for a time we were saved, although in the electric light Mr. Pierce was a good bit less like Dicky Carter than he had seemed to be in the spring-house by the fire.

Well, "Sufficient unto the day is the evil thereof."

Everybody went to bed early. Mr. Thoburn came over and bought a cigar on his way up-stairs, and he was as gloomy as he had been cheerful before.

"Well," I said, "I guess you won't put a dancing floor in the dining-room just yet, Mr. Thoburn."

"I'm not in a hurry," he snapped. "It's only January, and I don't want the place until May. I'll get it when I'm ready for it. I had a good look at young Carter, and he's got too square a jaw to run a successful neurasthenics' home."

I went to the pantry myself at ten o'clock and fixed a tray of supper for Mr. Pierce. He would need all his strength the next day, and a man can't travel far on buttered pop-corn. I found some chicken and got a bottle of the old doctor's wine—I had kept the key of his wine-cellar since he died—and carried the tray up to Mr. Pierce's sitting-room. He had the old doctor's suite.

The door was open an inch or so, and as I was about to knock I heard a girl's voice. It was Miss Patty!

"How can you deny it?" she was saying angrily. "I dare say you will even deny that you ever saw this letter before!"

There was a minute's pause while I suppose he looked at the letter.

"I never did!" he said solemnly.

There had been a queer sound all along, but now I made it out. Some one else was in the room, sniveling and crying.

"My poor lamb!" it whimpered. And I knew it was Mrs. Hutchins, Miss Patty's old nurse.

"Perhaps," said Miss Patty, "you also deny that you were in Ohio the day before yesterday."

"I was in Ohio, but I positively assert—"

"I'll send for the police, that's what I'll do!" Mrs. Hutchins said, with a burst of rage, and her chair creaked. "How can I ever tell your father?"

"You'll do nothing of the sort," said Miss Patty. "Do you want the whole story in the papers? Isn't it awful enough as it is? Mr. Carter, I have asked my question twice now and I am waiting for an answer."

"But I don't know the answer!" he said miserably. "I—I assure you, I'm absolutely in the dark. I don't know what's in the letter. I—I haven't always done what I should, I dare say, but my conduct in the state of Ohio during the last few weeks has been without stain—unless I've forgotten—but if it had been anything very heinous, I'd remember, don't you think?"

Somebody crossed the room, and a paper rustled.

"Read that!" said Miss Patty's voice. And then silence for a minute.

"Good lord!" exclaimed Mr. Pierce.

"Do you deny that?"

"Absolutely!" he said firmly. "I—I have never even heard of the Reverend Dwight Johnstone—"

There was a scream from Mrs. Hutchins, and a creak as she fell into her chair again.

"Your father!" she said, over and over. "What can we say to your father?"

"And that is all you will say?" demanded Miss Patty scornfully. "'You don't know;' 'there's a mistake;' 'you never saw the letter before!' Oh, if I were only a man!"

"I'll tell you what we'll do," Mr. Pierce said, with something like hope in his voice. "We'll send for Mr. Van Alstyne! That's the thing, of course. I'll send for—er—Jim."

Mr. Van Alstyne's name is Sam, but nobody noticed.

"Mr. Van Alstyne!" repeated Miss Patty in a dazed way.

I guessed it was about time to make a diversion, so I knocked and walked in with the tray, and they all glared at me. Mrs. Hutchins was collapsed in a chair, holding a wet handkerchief to her eyes, and one side of her cap was loose and hanging down. Miss Patty was standing by a table, white and angry, and Mr. Pierce was about a yard from her, with the letter in his hands. But he was looking at her.

"I've brought your supper, Mr. Carter," I began. Then I stopped and stared at Miss Patty and Mrs. Hutchins. "Oh," I said.

"Thank you," said Mr. Pierce, very uncomfortable. "Just put it down anywhere."

I stalked across the room and put it on the table. Then I turned and looked at Mrs. Hutchins.

"I'm sorry," I said, "but it's one of the rules of this house that guests don't come to these rooms. They're strictly private. It isn't MY rule, ladies, but if you will step down to the parlor—"

Mrs. Hutchins' face turned purple. She got up in a hurry.

"I'm here with Miss Jennings on a purely personal matter," she said furiously. "How dare you turn us out?"

"Nonsense, Minnie!" said Miss Patty. "I'll go when I'm ready."

"Rule of the house," I remarked, and going over to the door I stood holding it open. There wasn't any such rule, but I had to get them out; they had Mr. Pierce driven into a corner and yelling for help.

"There is no such rule and you know it, Minnie!" Miss Patty said angrily. "Come, Nana! We're not learning anything, and there's nothing to be done until morning, anyhow. My head's whirling."

Mrs. Hutchins went out first.

"The first thing I'D do if I owned this place, I'd get rid of that red-haired girl," she snapped to Mr. Pierce. "If you want to know why there are fewer guests here every year, I'll tell you. SHE'S the reason!" Then she flounced out with her head up.

That was pure piffle. The real reason, as every thinking person knows, is Christian Science. It's cheaper and more handy. And now that it isn't heresy to say it, the spring being floored over, I reckon that most mineral springs cure by suggestion. Also, of course, if a man's drinking four gallons of lithia water a day, he's so saturated that if he does throw in anything alcoholic or indigestible, it's too busy swimming for its life to do any harm.

Mr. Pierce took a quick step toward Miss Patty and looked down at her.

"About—what happened down-stairs to-night," he stammered, with the unhappiest face I ever saw on a man, "I—I've been ready to knock my fool head off ever since. It was a mistake—a—"

"My letter, please," said Miss Patty coolly, looking back at him without a blink.

"Please don't look like that!" he begged. "I came in suddenly out of the darkness, and you—"

"My letter, please!" she said again, raising her eyebrows.

He gave up trying then. He held out the letter and she took it and went out with her head up and scorn in the very way she trailed her skirt over the door-sill. But I'm no fool; it didn't need the way he touched the door-knob where she had been holding it, when he closed the door after her, to tell me what ailed him.

He was crazy about her from the minute he saw her, and he hadn't a change of linen or a cent to his name. And she, as you might say, on the ragged edge of royalty, with queens and princes sending her stomachers and tiaras until she'd hardly need clothes! Well, a cat may look at a king.

He went over to the fireplace, where I was putting his coffee to keep it hot, and looked down at me.

"I've a suspicion, Minnie," he said, "that, to use a vulgar expression, I've bitten off more than I can chew in this little undertaking, and that I'm in imminent danger of choking to death. Do you know anybody, a friend of Miss er—Jennings, named Dorothy?"

"She's got a younger sister of that name," I said, with a sort of chill going over me. "She's in boarding-school now."

"Oh, no, she's not!" he remarked, picking up the coffee-pot. "It seems that I met her on the train somewhere or other the day before yesterday, and ran off with her and married her!"

I sat back on the rug speechless.

"You should have warned me, Minnie," he went on, growing more cheerful over his chicken and coffee. "I came up here to-night, the proud possessor of a bunch of keys, a patent folding cork-screw and a pocket, automobile road map. Inside two hours I have a sanatorium and a wife. At this rate, Minnie, before morning I may reasonably hope to have a family."

I sat where I was on the floor and stared into the fire. Don't tell me the way of the wicked is hard; the wicked get all the fun there is out of life, and as far as I can see, it's the respectable "in at ten o'clock and up at seven" part of the wicked's family that has all the trouble and does the worrying.

"If we could only keep it hidden for a few days!" I said. "But, of course, the papers will get it, and just now, with columns every day about Miss Patty's clothes—"

"Her what?"

"And all the princes of the blood sending presents, and the king not favoring it very much—"

"What are you talking about?"

"About Miss Jennings' wedding. Don't you read the newspaper?"

He hadn't really known who she was up to that minute. He put down the tray and got up.

"I—I hadn't connected her with the—the newspaper Miss Jennings," he said, and lighted a cigarette over the lamp. Something in his face startled me, I must say.

"You're not going to give up now?" I asked. I got up and put my hand on his arm, and I think he was shaking. "If you do, I'll—I'll go out and drown myself, head down, in the spring."

He had been going to run away—I saw it then—but he put a hand over mine. Then he looked at the door where Miss Patty had gone out and gave himself a shake.

"I'll stay," he said. "We'll fight it out on this line if it takes all summer, Minnie." He stood looking into the fire, and although I'm not fond of men, knowing, as I have explained, a great deal about their stomachs and livers and very little about their hearts, there was something about Mr. Pierce that made me want to go up and pat him on the head like a little boy. "After all," he said, "what's blue blood to good red blood?"

Which was almost what the bishop had said!

CHAPTER VIII

AND MR. MOODY INDIGESTION

Mr. Moody took indigestion that night—not but that he always had it, but this was worse—and Mrs. Moody came to my room about two o'clock and knocked at the door.

"You'd better come," she said. "There's no doctor, and he's awful bad. Blames you, too; he says you made him take a salt rub."

"My land," I snapped, trying to find my bedroom slippers, "I didn't make him take clam chowder for supper, and that's what's the matter with him. He's going on a strained rice diet, that's what he's going to do. I've got to have my sleep."

She was waiting in the hall in her kimono, and holding a candle. Anybody could see she'd been crying. As she often said to me, of course she was grateful that Mr. Moody didn't drink—no one knew his virtues better than she did. But her sister married a man who went on a terrible bat twice a year, and all the rest of the time he was humble and affable trying to make up for it. And sometimes she thought if Mr. Moody would only take a little whisky when he had these attacks—! I'd rather be the wife of a cheerful drunkard any time than have to live with a cantankerous saint. Miss Cobb and I had had many a fight over it, but at that time there wasn't much likelihood of either of us being called on to choose.

Well, we went down to Mr. Moody's room, and he was sitting up in bed with his knees drawn up to his chin and a hot-water bottle held to him.

"Look at your work, woman," he said to me when I opened the door.

"I'm dying!"

"You look sick," I said, going over to the bed. It never does to cross them when they get to the water-bottle stage. "The pharmacy clerk's gone to a dance over at Trimble's, but I guess I can find you some whisky."

"Do have some whisky, George," begged Mrs. Moody, remembering her brother-in-law.

"I never touch the stuff and you both know it," he snarled. He had a fresh pain just then and stopped, clutching up the bottle. "Besides," he finished, when it was over, "I haven't got any whisky."

Well, to make a long story short, we got him to agree to some whisky from the pharmacy, with a drop of peppermint in it, if he could wash it down with spring water so it wouldn't do him any harm.

"There isn't any spring water in the house," I said, losing my temper a little, "and I'm not going out there in my bedroom slippers, Mr. Moody. I don't see why your eating what you shouldn't needs to give me pneumonia."

Mrs. Moody was standing beside the bed, and I saw her double chin begin to work. If you have ever seen a fat woman, in a short red kimono holding a candle by, a bed, and crying, you know how helpless she looks.

"Don't go, Minnie," she sniffled. "It would be too awful. If you are afraid you could take the poker."

"I'm not going!" I declared firmly. "It's—it's dratted idiocy, that's all. Plain water would do well enough. There's a lot of people think whisky is poison with water, anyhow. Where's the pitcher?"

Oh, yes, I went. I put on some stockings of Mrs. Moody's and a petticoat and a shawl and started. It was when I was in the pharmacy looking for the peppermint that I first noticed my joint again. A joint like that's a blessing or a curse, the way you look at it.

I found the peppermint and some whisky and put them on the stairs. Then I took my pitcher and lantern and started for the spring-house. It was still snowing, and part of the time Mrs. Moody's stockings were up to their knees. The wind was blowing hard, and when I rounded the corner of the house my lantern went out. I stood there in the storm, with the shawl flapping, thanking heaven I was a single woman, and about ready to go back and tell Mr. Moody what I thought of him when I looked toward the spring-house.

At first I thought it was afire, then I saw that the light was coming from the windows. Somebody was inside, with a big fire and all the lights going.

I'd had tramps sleep all night in the spring-house before, and once they left a card by the spring: "Water, water everywhere and not a drop to drink!" So I started out through the snow on a half run. By the bridge over Hope Springs Creek I slipped and fell, and I heard the pitcher smash to bits on the ice below. But as soon as I could move I went on again. That spring-house had been my home for a good many years, and the tramp didn't live who could spend the night there if I knew it.

I realized then that I should have taken the poker. I went over cautiously to one of the windows, wading in deep snow to get there—and if you have ever done that in a pair of bedroom slippers you can realize the state of my mind—and looked in.

There were three chairs drawn up in a row in front of the fire, with my bearskin hearth-rug on them to make a couch, and my shepherd's plaid shawl folded at one end for a pillow. And stretched on that with her long sealskin coat laid over her was Dorothy Jennings, Miss Patty's younger sister! She was alone, as far as I could see, and she was leaning on her elbow with her cheek in her hand, staring at the fire. Just then the door into the pantry opened and out came Mr. Dick himself.

"Were you calling, honey?" he said, coming over and looking down at her.

"You were such a long time!" says she, glancing up under her lashes at him. "I—I was lonely!"

"Bless you," says Mr. Dick, stooping over her. "What did I ever do without you?"

I could have told her a few things he did, but by that time it was coming over me pretty strong that here was the real Dicky Carter and that I had an extra one on my hands. The minute I looked at this one I knew that nobody but a blind man would mistake one for the other, and Mr. Thoburn wasn't blind. I tell you I stood out in that snow-bank and perspired!

When I looked again Mr. Dick was on his knees by the row of chairs, and Miss Dorothy—Mrs. Dicky, of course—was running her fingers through his hair.

"Minnie used to keep apples and things in the pantry," he said, "but she must be growing stingy in her old age; there's not a bite there."

"I'm not so very hungry when I have you!" cooed Mrs. Dicky.

"But you can't eat me." He brought her hand down from his hair—I may be stingy in my old age, but I've learned a few things, and one is that a man feels like a fool with his hair rumpled, and I can tell the degree of a woman's experience by the way she lets his top hair alone—and pretended to bite it, her hand, of course. "Although I could eat you," he said. "I'd like to take a bite out of your throat right there."

Well, it was no place for me unless they knew I was around. I waded around to the door and walked in, and there was a grand upsetting of the sealskin coat and my shepherd's plaid shawl. Mr. Dick jumped to his feet and Mrs. Dick sat bolt upright and stared at me over the backs of the chairs.

"Minnie!" cried Mr. Dick. "As I'm a married man, it's Minnie herself; Minnie, the guardian angel! The spirit of the place! Dorothy, don't you remember Minnie?"

She came toward me with her hand out. She was a pretty little thing, not so beautiful as Miss Patty, but with a nice way about her.

"I'm awfully glad to see you again," she said. "Of course I remember—why you are hardly dressed at all! You must be frozen!"

I went over to the fire and emptied my bedroom slippers of snow. Then I sat down and looked at them both.

"Frozen!" repeated I; "I'm in a hot sweat. If you two children meant to come, why in creation didn't you come in time?"

"We did," replied Mr. Dick, promptly. "We crawled under the wire fence into the deer park at five minutes to twelve. The will said 'Be on the ground,' and I was—flat on the ground!"

"We've had the police," I said, drearily enough. "I wouldn't live through another day like yesterday for a hundred dollars."

"We were held up by the snow," he explained. "We got a sleigh to come over in, but we walked up the hill and came here. I don't mind saying that my wife's people don't know about this yet, and we're going to lay low until we've cooked up some sort of a scheme to tell them." Then he came over and put his hand on my shoulder.

"Poor old Minnie!" he said; "honest, I'm sorry. I've been a hard child to raise, haven't I? But that's all over, Minnie. I've got an incentive now, and it's 'steady, old boy,' for me from now. You and I will run the place and run it right."

"I don't want to!" I retorted, holding my bedroom slippers to steam before the fire. "I'm going to buy out Timmon's candy store and live a quiet life, Mr. Dick. This place is making me old."

"Nonsense! We're going to work together, and we'll make this the busiest spot in seven counties. Dorothy and I have got it all planned out and we've got some corking good ideas." He put his hands in his pockets and strutted up and down. "It's the day of advertising, you know, Minnie," he said. "You've got to have the goods, and then you've got to let people know you've got the goods. What would you say to a shooting-gallery in the basement, under the reading-room?"

"Fine!" I said, with sarcasm, turning my slippers. "If things got too quiet that would wake them up a bit, and we could have a balloon ascension on Saturdays!"

"Not an ascension," said he, with my bitterness going right over his head. "Nothing sensational, Minnie. That's the way with women; they're always theatrical. But what's the matter with a captive balloon, and letting fresh-air cranks sleep in a big basket bed—say, at five hundred feet? Or a thousand—a thousand would be better. The air's purer."

"With a net below," says I, "in case they should turn over and fall out of bed! It's funny nobody ever thought of it before!"

"Isn't it?" exclaimed Mrs. Dick. "And we've all sorts of ideas. Dick—Mr. Carter has learned of a brand new cocktail for the men—"

"A lulu!" he broke in.

"And I'm going around to read to the old ladies and hold their hands—"

"You'll have to chloroform them first," I put in. "Perhaps it would be better to give the women the cocktail and hold the men's hands."

"Oh, if you're going to be funny!" Mr. Dick said savagely, "we'll not tell you any more. I've been counting on you, Minnie. You've been here so long. You know," he said to his wife, "when I was a little shaver I thought Minnie had webbed-feet—she was always on the bank, like a duck. You ARE a duck, Minnie," he says to me; "a nice red-headed duck! Now don't be quirky and spoil everything."

I couldn't be light-hearted to save my life.

"Your sister's been wild all day," I told Mrs. Dick. "She got your letter to-day—yesterday—but I don't think she's told your father yet."

"What!" she screeched, and caught at the mantelpiece to hold herself. "Not Pat!" she said, horrified, "and father! Here!"

Well, I listened while they told me. They hadn't had the faintest idea that Mr. Jennings and Miss Patty were there at the sanatorium. The girl had been making a round of visits in the Christmas holidays, and instead of going back to school she'd sent a forged excuse and got a month off—she hadn't had any letters, of course. The plan had been not to tell anybody but her sister until Mr. Dick had made good at the sanatorium.

"The idea was this, Minnie," said Mr. Dick. "Old—I mean Mr. Jennings is—is not well; he has a chronic indisposition—"

"Disposition, I call it," put in Mr. Jennings' daughter.

"And he's apt to regard my running away with Dorothy when I haven't a penny as more of an embezzlement than an elopement."

"Fiddle!" exclaimed Mrs. Dick. "I asked you to marry me, and now they're here and have to spoil it all."

The thought of her father and his disposition suddenly overpowered her and she put her yellow head on the back of a chair and began to cry.

"I—I can't tell him!" she sobbed. "I wrote to Pat,—why doesn't Pat tell him? I'm going back to school."

"You'll do nothing of the sort. You're a married woman now, and where I go you go. My country is your country, and my sanatorium is your sanatorium." He was in a great rage.

But she got up and began trying to pull on her fur coat, and her jaw was set. She looked like her father for a minute.

"Where are you going?" he asked, looking scared.

"Anywhere. I'll go down to the station and take the first train, it doesn't matter where to." She picked up her muff, but he went over and stood against the door.

"Not a step without me!" he declared. "I'll go with you, of course; you know that. I'm not afraid of your father: I'd as soon as not go in and wake him now and tell him the whole thing—that you've married a chap who isn't worth the butter on his bread, who can't buy you kid gloves—"

"But you will, as soon as the sanatorium succeeds!" she put in bravely. She put down her muff. "Don't tell him to-night, anyhow. Maybe Pat will think of some way to break it to him. She can do a lot with father."

"I hope she can think of some way to break another Richard Carter to the people in the house," I said tartly.

"Another Richard Carter!" they said together, and then I told them about how we had waited and got desperate, and how we'd brought in Mr. Pierce at the last minute and that he was asleep now at the house. They roared. To save my life I couldn't see that it was funny. But when I came to the part about Thoburn being there, and his having had a good look at Mr. Pierce, and that he was waiting around with his jaws open to snap up the place when it fell under the hammer, Mr. Dick stopped laughing and looked serious.

"Lord deliver us from our friends!" he said. "Between you and Sam, you've got things in a lovely mess, Minnie. What are you going to do about it now?"

"It's possible we can get by Thoburn," I said. "You can slip in to-night, we can get Mr. Pierce out—Lord knows he'll be glad to go—and Miss Dorothy can go back to school. Then, later, when you've got things running and are making good—"

"I'm not going back to school," she declared, "but I'll go away; I'll not stand in your way, Dicky." She took two steps toward the door and waited for him to stop her.

"Nonsense, Minnie," he exclaimed angrily and put his arm around her, "I won't be separated from my wife. You got me into this scrape, and—"

"I didn't marry you!" I retorted. "And I'm not responsible for your father-in-law's disposition."

"You'll have to help us out," he finished.

"What shall I do? Murder Mr. Jennings?" I asked bitterly. "If you expect me to suggest that you both go to the house, and your wife can hide in your rooms—"

"Why not?" asked Mr. Dick.

Well, I sat down again and explained patiently that it would get out among the servants and cause a scandal, and that even if it didn't I wasn't going to have any more deception: I had enough already. And after a while they saw it as I did, and agreed to wait and see Miss Patty before they decided. They wanted to have her wakened at once, but I refused, although I agreed to bring her out first thing in the morning.

"But you can't stay here," I said. "There'll be Miss Cobb at nine o'clock, and the man comes to light the fire at eight."

"We could go to the old shelter-house on the golf links," suggested Mr. Dick, looking me square in the eye. I took the hint, and Mrs. Dicky never knew he had been hidden there before.

"Nobody ever goes near it in winter." So I put on my slippers again and we started through the snow across the golf links, Mr. Dick carrying a bundle of firewood, and I leading the way with my lantern. Twice I went into a drift to my waist, and once a rabbit bunted into me head on, and would have scared me into a chill if I hadn't been shaking already. The two behind me were cheerful enough. Mr. Dick pointed out the general direction of the deer park which hides the shelter-house from the sanatorium, and if you'll believe it, with snow so thick I had to scrape it off the lantern every minute or so, those children planned to give something called A Midsummer Night's Dream in the deer park among the trees in the spring, to entertain the patients.

"I wish to heaven I'd wake up and find all THIS a dream," I called back over my shoulder. But they were busy with costumes and getting some folks they knew from town to take the different parts and they never even heard me. The last few yards they snowballed each other and me. I tell you I felt a hundred years old.

We got into the shelter-house by my crawling through a window, and when we had lighted the fire and hung up the lantern, it didn't seem so bad. The place had been closed since summer, and it seemed colder than outside, but those two did the barn dance then and there. There were two rooms, and Mr. Dick had always used the back one to hide in. It's a good thing Mrs. Dick was not a suspicious person. Many a woman would have wondered when she saw him lift a board in the floor and take out a rusty tin basin, a cake of soap, a moldy towel, a can of sardines, a tooth-brush and a rubber carriage robe to lay over the rafters under the hole in the roof. But it's been my experience that the first few days of married life women are blind because they want to be and after that because they have to be.

It was about four when I left them, sitting on a soap box in front of the fire toasting sardines on the end of Mr. Dick's walking-stick. Mrs. Dick made me put on her sealskin coat, and I took the lantern, leaving them in the firelight. They'd gone back to the captive balloon idea and were wondering if they couldn't get it copyrighted!

I took a short cut home, crawling through the barbed-wire fence and going through the deer park. I was too tired and cold to think. I stumbled down the hill to the house, and just before I got to the corner I heard voices, and the shuffling of feet through the snow. The next instant a lantern came around the corner of the house. Mr. Thoburn was carrying it, and behind him were the bishop, Mike the bath man, and Mr. Pierce.

"It's like that man Moody," the bishop was saying angrily, "to send the girl—"

"Piffle!" snarled Mr. Thoburn. "If ever a woman was able to take care of herself—" And then they saw me, and they all stopped and stared.

"Good gracious, girl!" said the bishop, with his dressing-gown blowing out straight behind him in the wind. "We thought you'd been buried in a drift!"

"I don't see why!" I retorted defiantly. "Can't I go out to my own spring-house without having a posse after me to bring me back?"

"Ordinarily," said Mr. Thoburn, with his snaky eyes on me, "I think I may say that you might go almost anywhere without my turning out to recover you. But Mrs. Moody is having hysterics."

Mrs. Moody! I'd forgotten the Moodys!

"She is convinced that you have drowned yourself, head down, in the spring," Mr. Pierce said in his pleasant way. "You've been gone two hours, you know."

He took my arm and turned me toward the house. I was dazed.

"In answer to your urgent inquiry," Mr. Thoburn called after me, disagreeably, "Mr. Moody has not died. He is asleep. But, by the way, where's the spring water?"

I didn't answer him; I couldn't. We went into the house; Mrs. Moody and Miss Cobb were sitting on the stairs. Mrs. Moody had been crying, and Miss Cobb was feeding her the whisky I had left, with a teaspoon. She had had a half tumblerful already and was quite maudlin. She ran to me and put her arms around me.

"I thought I was a murderess!" she cried. "Oh, the thought! Blood on my soul! Why, Minnie Waters, wherever did you get that sealskin coat!"

CHAPTER IX

DOLLY, HOW COULD YOU?

I lay down across my bed at six o'clock that morning, but I was too tired and worried to sleep, so at seven I got up and dressed.

I was frightened when I saw myself in the glass. My eyes looked like burnt holes in a blanket. I put on two pairs of stockings and heavy shoes, for I knew I was going to do the Eskimo act again that day and goodness knows how many days more, and then I went down and knocked at the door of Miss Patty's room. She hadn't been sleeping either. She called to me in an undertone to come in, and she was lying propped up with pillows, with something pink around her shoulders and the night lamp burning beside the bed. She had a book in her hand, but all over the covers and on the table at her elbow were letters in the blue foreign envelopes with the red and black and gold seal.

I walked over to the foot of the bed.

"They're here," I said.

She sat up, and some letters slid to the floor.

"THEY'RE here!" she repeated. "Do you mean Dorothy?"

"She and her husband. They came last night at five minutes to twelve. Their train was held up by the blizzard and they won't come in until they see you. They're hiding in the shelter-house on the golf links."

I think she thought I was crazy: I looked it. She hopped out of bed and closed the door into her sitting-room—Mrs. Hutchins' room opened off it—and then she came over and put her hand on my arm.

"Will you sit down and try to tell me just what you mean?" she said. "How can my sister and her—her wretch of a husband have come last night at midnight when I saw Mr. Carter myself not later than ten o'clock?"

Well, I had to tell her then about who Mr. Pierce was and why I had to get him, and she understood almost at once. She was the most understanding girl I ever met. She saw at once what Mr. Sam wouldn't have known in a thousand years—that I wanted to save the old place not to keep my position—but because I'd been there so long, and my father before me, and had helped to make it what it was and all that. And she stood there in her nightgown—she who was almost a princess—and listened to me, and patted me on the shoulder when I broke down, telling her about Thoburn and the summer hotel.

"But here I am," I finished, "telling you about my troubles and forgetting what I came for. You'll have to go out to the shelter-house, Miss Patty. And I guess you're expected to fix it up with your father."

She stopped unfastening her long braids of hair.

"Certainly I'll go to the shelter-house," she said, "and I'll shake a little sense into Dorothy Jennings—the abominable little idiot! But they needn't think I'm going to help them with father; I wouldn't if I could, and I can't. He won't speak to me. I'm in disgrace, Minnie." She gave her hair a shake, twisted it into a rope and then a knot, and stuck a pin in it. It was lovely: I wish Miss Cobb could have seen her. "You've known father for years, Minnie: have you ever known him to be so—so—"

"Devilish" was the word she meant, but I finished for her.

"Unreasonable?" I said. "Well, once before when you were a little girl, he put his cane through a window in the spring-house, because he thought it needed air. The spring-house, of course, not the cane."

"Exactly," she said, looking around the room, "and now he's putting a cane through every plan I have made. Do you see my heavy boots?"

"It's like this," I remarked, bringing the boots from outside the door, "if he's swallowed the prince and is choking on the settlement question he might as well get over it. All those foreigners expect pay for taking a wife. Didn't the chef here want to marry Tillie, the diet cook, and didn't he want her to turn over the three hundred dollars she had in the bank, and her real estate, which was a sixth interest in a cemetery lot? But Tillie stuck it out and he wouldn't take her without."

"It isn't quite the same, Minnie," she said, sitting down on the floor to put on her stockings.

"The principle's the same," I retorted, "and if you ask me—"

"I haven't," she said disagreeably, "and when you begin to argue, Minnie, you make my head ache."

"I have had a heartache for a week," I snapped, "let alone heartburn, and I'll be glad when the Jennings family is safely married and I can sleep at night."

I was hurt. I went out and shut the door behind me, but I stopped in the hall and went back.

"I forgot to say," I began, and stopped. She was still sitting on the floor, trying to put her heavy boots on, and crying all over them.

"Stop that instantly," I said, and jerked her shoes from her. "Get into a chair and let me put them on. And if you will wait a jiffy I'll bring you a cup of coffee. I'm not even a Christian in the morning until I've had my coffee."

"You haven't had it yet, have you?" she asked, and we laughed together, rather shaky. But as I buttoned her shoes I saw her eyes going toward the blue letters on the bed.

"Oh, Minnie," she said, "if you only knew how peculiar they are in Europe! They'll never allow a sanatorium in the family!"

"I guess a good many would be the better for having one close," I said.

Well, I left her to get dressed and went to the kitchens. Tillie was there getting the beef tea ready for the day, but none of the rest was around. They knew the housekeeper was gone, but I guess they'd forgotten that I was still on hand. I put a kettle against the electric bell that rings in the chef's room so it would keep on ringing and went on into the diet kitchen.

"Tillie," I said, "can you trust me?"

She looked up from her beef.

"Whether I can or not, I always have," she answered.

"Well, can I trust you? That's more to the point."

She put down her knife and came over to me, with her hands on her hips.

"I don't know what you're up to, Minnie," she said, "and I don't know that I care. But if you've forgotten the time I went to the city and brought you sulphur and the Lord only knows what for your old spring when you'd run short and were laid up with influenza—"

"Hush!" I exclaimed. "You needn't shout it. Tillie, I don't want you to ask me any questions, but I want four raw eggs in a basket, a pot of coffee and cream, some fruit if you can get it when the chef unlocks the refrigerator room, and bread and butter. They can make their own toast."

"They?" she said, with her mouth open.

But I didn't explain any more. I had found Tillie about a year before, frying sausages at the railroad station, and made her diet cook at the sanatorium. Mrs. Wiggins hadn't wanted her, but, as I told the old doctor at the time, we needed somebody in the kitchen to keep an eye on things for us. It was through Tillie that we discovered that the help were having egg-nog twice a day, with eggs as scarce as hens' teeth, and the pharmacy clerk putting in a requisition for more whisky every week.

Well, I scribbled a note to Mr. Van Alstyne, telling what had happened, and put it under his door, and then I met Miss Patty in the hall by the billiard room and I gave her some coffee from the basket, in the sun parlor. It was still dark, although it was nearly eight o'clock, and nobody saw us go out together. Just as we left I heard the chef in the kitchen bawling out that he'd murder whoever put the kettle against the bell, and Tillie saying it must have dropped off the hook and landed there.

We went to the spring-house first, to avoid suspicion, and then across back of the deer park to the shelter-house. It was still snowing, but not so much, and the tracks we had made early in the morning were still there, mine off to one side alone, and the others close together and side by side. There was a whole history in those snow tracks, mine alone and kind of offish, and the others cuddling together. It made me lonely to look at them.

I remember wishing I'd taught school, as I was educated to; woman wasn't made to live alone, and most school-teachers get married.

Miss Patty did not say much. She was holding her chin high and looking rather angry and determined. At the spring-house I gave her the basket and took an armful of fire-wood myself. I knew Mr. Dick would never think of it until the fire was out.

They were both asleep in the shelter-house. He was propped up against the wall on a box, with the rubber carriage robe around him, and she was lying by the fire, with Mrs. Moody's shawl over her and her muff under her head. Miss Patty stood in the doorway for an instant. Then she walked over and, leaning down, shook her sister by the arm.

"Dorothy!" she said. "Wake up, you wretched child!" And shook her again.

Mrs. Dicky groaned and yawned, and opened her eyes one at a time.

But when she saw it was Miss Patty she sat up at once, looking dazed and frightened.

"You needn't pinch me, Pat!" she said, and at that Mr. Dick wakened and jumped up, with the carriage robe still around him.

"Oh, Dolly, Dolly!" said Miss Patty suddenly, dropping on her knees beside Mrs. Dicky, "what a bad little girl you are! What a thing for you to do! Think of father and Aunt Honoria!"

"I shan't," retorted Mrs. Dicky decidedly. "I'm not going to spoil my honeymoon like that. For heaven's sake, Pat, don't cry. I'm not dead. Dick, this is my sister, Patricia."

Miss Pat looked at him, but she didn't bow. She gave him one look, from his head to his heels.

"Dolly, how COULD you!" she said, and got up.

It wasn't very comfortable for Mr. Dick, but he took it much better than I expected. He went over and gave his wife a hand to help her up, and still holding hers, he turned to Miss Patty.

"You are perfectly right," he said, "I don't see how she could myself. The more you know of me the more you'll wonder. But she did; we're up against that."

He grinned at Miss Patty, and after a minute Miss Patty smiled back. But it wasn't much of a smile. I was unpacking the breakfast, putting the coffee-pot on the fire and getting ready to cook the eggs and make toast. But I was watching, too. Suddenly Mrs. Dick made a dive for Miss Patty and threw her arms around her.

"You darling!" she cried. "I'm so glad to see you again—Pat, you'll tell father, won't you? He'll take it from you. If I tell him he'll have apoplexy or something."

But Miss Patty set her pretty mouth—both those girls have their father's mouth—and held her sister out at arm's length and looked at her.

"Listen," she said. "Do you know what you have done to me? Do you know that when father knows this he's going to annul the marriage or have Mr. Carter arrested for kidnaping or abduction?—whatever it is." Mrs. Dick puckered her face to cry, and Mr. Dick took a step forward, but Miss Patty waved him off. "You know father as well as I do, Dolly. You know what he is, and lately he's been awful. He's not well—it's his liver again—and he won't listen to anything. Why, the Austrian ambassador came up here, all this distance, to talk about the etiquette of the—of my wedding, something about precedence, and he wouldn't even see him."

"He can't annul it," said Mr. Dick angrily. "I'm of age. And I can support my wife, too, or will be able—soon."

"Dolly's not of age," said Miss Patty wearily. "I've sat up all night figuring it out. He's going to annul the marriage, or he'll make a scandal anyhow, and that's just as bad. Dolly,"—she turned to her sister imploringly—"Dolly, I can't have a scandal now. You know how Oskar's people have taken this, anyhow; they've given in, because he insisted, but they don't want me, and if there's a lot of notoriety now the emperor will send him to Africa or some place, and—"

"I wish they would!" Mrs. Carter burst out suddenly. "I hate the whole thing. They only tolerate you—us—for our money. You needn't look at me like that; Oskar may be all right, but his mother and sisters are hateful—simply hateful!"

"I'll not be with them."

"No, but they'll be with you." Mrs. Dicky walked over to the window and looked out, dabbing her eyes. "You've been everything to me, Pat, and I'm so happy now—I'd rather be here on a soap box with Dick than on a throne or a dais or whatever you'll have to sit on over there, with Oskar. I want to be happy—and you won't. Look at Alice Thorne and her duke!"

"If you really want me to be happy," Miss Patty said, going over to her, "you'll go back to school until the wedding is over."

"I won't leave Dicky." She swung around and gave Mr. Dick an adoring glance, and Miss Patty looked discouraged.

"Take him with you," she said. "Isn't there some place near where he could stay, and telephone you now and then?"

"Telephone!" said Mrs. Dick scornfully.

"Can't leave," Mr. Dick objected. "Got to be on the property."

Miss Patty shrugged her shoulders and turned to go. "You're both perfectly hopeless," she said. "I'll go and tell father, Dorothy, but you know what will happen. You'll be back in school at Greenwich by to-night, and your—husband will probably be under arrest." She opened the door, but I dropped the toast I was making and ran after her.

"If he is arrested," I said, "they'll have to keep him on the place. He can't leave."

She didn't say anything; she lifted her hand and looked at the ruby ring, and then she glanced back into the room where Mr. Dick and his wife were whispering together, and turned up her coat collar.

"I'm going," she said, and stepped into the snow. But they called her back in a hurry.

"Look here, Miss—Miss Patricia," Mr. Dick said, "why can't we stay here, where we are? It's very comfortable—that is, it's livable. There's plenty of fresh air, anyhow, and everybody's shouting for fresh air nowadays. They've got somebody to take my place in the house."

"And father needn't know a thing—you can fix that," broke in Mrs. Dick. "And after your wedding he will be in a better humor; he'll know it's over and not up to him any more."

Miss Patty came back to the shelter-house again and sat down on the soap box.

"We MIGHT carry it off," she said. "If I could only go back to town! But father is in one of his tantrums, and he won't go, or let me go. The idea!—with Aunt Honoria on the long-distance wire every day, having hysterics, and my clothes waiting to be tried on and everything. I'm desperate."

"And all sorts of things being arranged for you!" put in Mrs. Dick enviously. "And the family jewels being reset in Vienna for you and all that! It would be great—if you only didn't have to take Oskar with the jewels!"

Miss Patty frowned.

"You are not going to marry him," she said, with a glance at Mr. Dick, who, with his coat off, was lying flat on the floor, one arm down in the hole where the things had been hidden, trying to hook up a can of baked beans. "If it doesn't turn out well, you and father have certainly done your part in the way of warning. It's just as Aunt Honoria said; the family will make a tremendous row beforehand, but afterward, when it all turns out well, they'll take the credit."

Mr. Dick was busy with the beans and I was turning the eggs. Mrs. Dick went over to her sister and put her arm around her.

"That's right, Patty," she said, "you're more like mother than I am. I'm a Jennings all over—except that, heavens be praised, I've got the Sherwood liver. I guess I'm common plebeian, like dad, too. I'm plebeian enough, anyhow, to think there's been a lot too much about marriage settlements and the consent of the emperor in all this, and not enough about love."

I could have patted Mrs. Dicky on the back for that, and I almost upset the eggs into the fire. I'm an advocate of marrying for love every time, although a title and a bunch of family jewels thrown in wouldn't worry me.

"Do you want me to protest that the man who has asked me to marry him cares about me?" Miss Patty replied in an angry undertone. "Couldn't he have married a thousand other girls! Hadn't a marriage been arranged between him and the cousin—"

"I know all that," Mrs. Dicky said, and her voice sounded older than Miss Patty's, and motherly. "But—are you in love with him, Pat?"

"Certainly," Miss Patty said indignantly. "Don't be silly, Dolly."

At that instant Mr. Dick found the beans, and got up shouting that we'd have a meal fit for a prince—if princes ate anything so every day as baked beans. I put the eggs on a platter and poured the coffee, and we all sat around the soap box and ate. I wished that Miss Cobb could have seen me there— how they insisted on my having a second egg, and was my coffee cold, and wasn't I too close to the fire? It was Minnie here and Minnie there, and me next to Miss Patty on the floor, and she, as you may say, right next to royalty. I wished it could have been in the spring-house, with father's crayon enlargement looking down on us.

Everybody felt better for the meal, and we were sitting there laughing and talking and very cheerful when Mr. Van Alstyne opened the door and looked in. His face was stern, but when he saw us, with Miss Patty on her knees toasting a piece of bread and Mr. Dicky passing the tin basin as a finger-bowl, he stopped scowling and looked amused.

"They're here, Sallie," he called to his wife, and they both came in, covered with snow, and we had coffee and eggs all over again.

Well, they stayed for an hour, and Mr. Sam talked himself black in the face and couldn't get anywhere. For the Dickys refused to be separated, and Mrs. Dick wouldn't tell her father, and Miss Patty wouldn't do it for her, and the minute Mr. Sam made a suggestion that sounded rational Mrs. Dick would cry and say she didn't care to live, anyhow, and she wished she had died of ptomaine poisoning the time she ate the bad oysters at school.

So finally Mr. Sam gave up and said he washed his hands of the whole affair, and that he was going to make another start on his wedding journey, and if they wanted to be a pair of fools it wasn't up to him—only for heaven's sake not to cry about it. And then he wiped Mrs. Dicky's eyes and kissed her, she being, as he explained, his sister-in-law now and much too pretty for him to scold.

And when the Dickys found they were not going to be separated we had more coffee all around and everybody grew more cheerful.

Oh, we were very cheerful! I look back now and think how cheerful we were, and I shudder. It was strange that we hadn't been warned by Mr. Pierce's square jaw, but we were not. We sat around the fire and ate and laughed, and Mr. Dick arranged that Mr. Pierce should come out to him every evening for orders about the place if he accepted, and everybody felt he would—and I was to come at the same time and bring a basket of provisions for the next day. Of course, the instant Mr. Jennings left the young couple could go into the sanatorium as guests under another name and be comfortable. And as soon as the time limit was up, and the place was still running smoothly, they could declare the truth, claim the sanatorium, having fulfilled the conditions of the will, and confess to Mr. Jennings—over the long-distance wire.

Well, it promised well, I must say. Mr. Stitt left on the ten train that morning, looking lemon-colored and mottled. He insisted that he wasn't able to go, but Mr. Sam gave him a headache powder and put him on the train, anyhow.

Yes, as I say, it promised well. But we made two mistakes: we didn't count on Mr. Thoburn, and we didn't know Mr. Pierce. And who could have imagined that Mike the bath man would do as he did?

CHAPTER X

ANOTHER COMPLICATION

After luncheon, when everybody at Hope Springs takes a nap, we had another meeting at the shelter-house, this time with Mr. Pierce. He had spent the morning tramping over the hills with a gun and keeping out of the way of people, and what with three square meals, a good night's sleep and the exercise, he was looking a lot better. Seen in daylight, he had very dark hair and blue-gray eyes and a very square chin, although it had a sort of dimple in it. I used to wonder which won out, the dimple or the chin, but I wasn't long in finding out.

Well, he looked dazed when I took him to the shelter-house and he saw Mr. Dick and Mrs. Dick and the Mr. Sams and Miss Patty. They gave him a lawn-mower to sit on, and Mr. Sam explained the situation.

"I know it's asking a good bit, Mr. Pierce," he said, "and personally I can see only one way out of all this. Carter ought to go in and take charge, and his—er—wife ought to go back to school. But they won't have it, and—er—there are other reasons." He glanced at Miss Patty.

Mr. Pierce also glanced at Miss Patty. He'd been glancing at her at intervals of two seconds ever since she came in, and being a woman and having a point to gain, Miss Patty seemed to have forgotten the night before, and was very nice to him. Once she smiled directly at him, and whatever he was saying died in his throat of the shock. When she turned her head away he stared at the back of her neck, and when she looked at the fire he gazed at her profile, and always with that puzzled look, as if he hadn't yet come to believe that she was the newspaper Miss Jennings.

After everything had been explained to him, including Mr. Jennings' liver and disposition, she turned to him and said:

"We are in your hands, you see, Mr. Pierce. Are you going to help us?" And when she asked him that, it was plain to me that he was only sorry he couldn't die helping.

"If everybody agrees to it," he said, looking at her, "and you all think it's feasible and I can carry it off, I'm perfectly willing to try."

"Oh, it's feasible," Mr. Dick said in a relieved voice, getting up and beginning to strut up and down the room. "It isn't as though I'm beyond call. You can come out here and consult me if you get stuck. And then there's Minnie; she knows a good bit about the old place."

Mr. Sam looked at me and winked.

"Of course," said Mr. Dick, "I expect to retain control, you understand that, I suppose, Pierce? You can come out every day for instructions. I dare say sanatoriums are hardly your line."

Mr. Pierce was looking at Miss Patty and she knew it. When a woman looks as unconscious as she did it isn't natural.

"Eh—oh, well no, hardly," he said, coming to himself; "I've tried everything else, I believe. It can't be worse than carrying a bunch of sweet peas from garden to garden."

Mr. Dick stopped walking and turned suddenly to stare at Mr. Pierce.

"Sweet—what?" he said.

Everybody else was talking, and I was the only one who saw him change color.

"Sweet peas," said Mr. Pierce. "And that reminds me—I'd like to make one condition, Mr. Carter. I feel in a measure responsible for the company; most of them have gone back to New York, but the leading woman is sick at the hotel in Finleyville. I'd like to bring her here for two weeks to recuperate. I assure you, I have no interest in her, but I'm sorry for her; she's had the mumps."

"Mumps!" everybody said together, and Mr. Sam looked at his brother-in-law.

"Kid in the play got 'em, and they spread around," Mr. Pierce explained. "Nasty disease."

"Why, you've just had them, too, Dicky!" said his wife. They all turned to look at him, and I must say his expression was curious.

Luckily, I had the wit to knock over the breakfast basket, which was still there, and when we'd gathered up the broken china, Mr. Dick had got himself in hand.

"I'm sorry, old man," he said to Mr. Pierce, "but I'm not in favor of bringing Miss—the person you speak of—up to the sanatorium just now. Mumps, you know—very contagious, and all that."

"She's over that part," Mr. Pierce said; "she only needs to rest."

"Certainly—let her come," said Mrs. Dicky. "If they're as contagious as all that, you haven't been afraid of MY getting them."

"I—I'm not in favor of it," Mr. Dick insisted, looking obstinate. "The minute you bring an actress here you've got the whole place by the ears."

"Fiddlesticks!" said his sister. "Because any actress could set YOU by the ears—"

Mrs. Dick sat up suddenly.

"Certainly, if she isn't well bring her up," said Miss Patty. "Only—won't she know your name is not Carter?"

"She's discretion itself," Mr. Pierce said. "Her salary hasn't been paid for a month, and as I'm responsible, I'd be glad to see her looked after."

"I don't want her here. I'll—I'll pay her board at the hotel," Mr. Dick began, "only for heaven's sake, don't—"

He stopped, for every one was staring.

"Why in the world would you do that?" Miss Patty asked. "Don't be ridiculous. That's the only condition Mr. Pierce has made."

Mr. Dick stalked to the window and looked out, his hands in his pockets. I couldn't help being reminded of the time he had run away from school, when his grandfather found him in the shelter-house and gave him his choice of going back at once or reading medicine with him.

"Oh, bring her up! Bring her up!" he said without looking around. "If Pierce won't stay unless he can play the friend in need, all right. But don't come after me if the whole blamed sanatorium swells up with mumps and faints at the sight of a pickle."

That was Wednesday.

Things at the sanatorium were about the same on the surface. The women crocheted and wondered what the next house doctor would be like, and the men gambled at the slot-machines and played billiards and grumbled at the food and the management, and when they weren't drinking spring water they were in the bar washing away the taste of it. They took twenty minutes on the verandas every day for exercise and kept the house temperature at eighty. Senator Biggs was still fasting and Mrs. Biggs took to spending all day in the spring-house and turning pale every time she heard his voice. It was that day, I think, that I found the magazine with Upton Sinclair's article on fasting stuck fast in a snow-drift, as if it had been thrown violently.

Wednesday afternoon Miss Julia Summers came with three lap robes, a white lace veil and a French poodle in a sleigh and went to bed in one of the best rooms, and that night we started to move out furniture to the shelter-house.

By working almost all night we got the shelter-house fairly furnished, although we made a trail through the snow that looked like a fever chart. Toward daylight Mr. Sam dropped a wash-bowl on my toe and I went to bed with an arnica compress.

I limped out in time to be on hand before Miss Cobb got there, but what with a chilblain on my heel and hardly any sleep for two nights—not to mention my toe—I wasn't any too pleasant.

"It's my opinion you're overeating, Minnie," Miss Cobb said. "You're skin's a sight!"

"You needn't look at it," I retorted.

She burned the back of her neck just then and it was three minutes before she could speak. When she could she was considerably milder.

"Just give it a twist or two, Minnie, won't you?" she said, holding out the curler. "I haven't been able to sleep on the back of my head for three weeks."

Well, I curled her hair for her and she told me about Miss Summers being still shut in her room, and how she'd offered Mike an extra dollar to give the white poodle a Turkish bath—it being under the weather as to health—and how Mike had soaked the little beast for an hour in a tub of water, forgetting the sulphur, and it had come out a sort of mustard color, and how Miss Summers had had hysterics when she saw it.

"Mike dipped him in bluing to bleach him again, or rather 'her'—it's name is Arabella—" Miss Cobb said, "but all it did was to make it mottled like an Easter egg. Everybody is charmed. There were no dogs allowed while the old doctor lived. Things were different."

"Yes, things were different," I assented, limping over to heat the curler. "How—how does Mr. Carter get along?"

Miss Cobb put down her hand-mirror and sniffed.

"Well," she said, "goodness knows I'm no trouble maker, but somebody ought to tell that young man a few things. He's forever looking at the thermometer and opening windows. I declare, if I hadn't brought my woolen tights along I'd have frozen to death at breakfast. Everybody's complaining."

I put that away in my mind to speak about. It was only by nailing the windows shut and putting strips of cotton batting around the cracks that we'd ever been able to keep people there in the winter. I had my first misgiving then. Heaven knows I didn't realize what it was going to be.

Well, by the evening of that day things were going fairly well. Tillie brought out a basket every morning to me at the spring-house, fairly bursting with curiosity, and Mr. Sam got some canned stuff in Finleyville and took it after dark to the shelter-house. But after the second day Mrs. Dicky got tired holding a frying-pan over the fire and I had to carry out at least one hot meal a day.

They got their own breakfast in a chafing-dish, or rather he got it and carried it to her. And she'd sit on the edge of her cot, with her feet on the soap box—the floor was drafty—wrapped in a pink satin negligee with bands of brown fur on it, looking sweet and perfectly happy, and let him feed her boiled egg with a spoon. I took them some books—my Gray's Anatomy, and Jane Eyre and Molly Bawn, by The Duchess, and the newspapers, of course. They were full of talk about the wedding, and the suite the prince was bringing over with him, and every now and then a notice would say that Miss Dorothy Jennings, the bride's young sister, who was still in school and was not coming out until next year, would be her sister's maid of honor. And when they came to that, they would hug each other—or me, if I happened to be close—and act like a pair of children, which they were. Generally it would end up by his asking her if she wasn't sorry she wasn't back at Greenwich studying French conjugations and having a dance without any men on Friday nights, and she would say "Wretch!" and kiss him, and I'd go out and slam the door.

But there was something on Mr. Dick's mind. I hadn't known him for fourteen years for nothing. And the night Mr. Sam and I carried out the canned salmon and corn and tomatoes he walked back with me to the edge of the deer park, Mr. Sam having gone ahead.

"Now," I said, when we were out of ear-shot, "spit it out. I've been expecting it."

"Listen, Minnie," he answered, "is Ju—is Miss Summers still confined to her room?"

"No," I replied coldly. "Ju—Miss Summers was down to-night to dinner."

"Then she's seen Pierce," he said, "and he's told her the whole story and by to-morrow—"

"What?" I demanded, clutching his arm. "You wretched boy, don't tell me after all I've done."

"Oh, confound it, Minnie," he exclaimed, "it's as much your fault as mine. Couldn't you have found somebody else, instead of getting, of all things on earth, somebody from the Sweet Peas Company?"

"I see," I said slowly. "Then it WASN'T coincidence about the mumps!"

"Confounded kid had them," he said with bitterness. "Minnie, something's got to be done, and done soon. If you want the plain truth, Miss—er—Summers and I used to be friends—and—well, she's suing me for breach of promise. Now for heaven's sake, Minnie, don't make a fuss—"

But my knees wouldn't hold me. I dropped down in a snow-drift and covered my face.

CHAPTER XI

MISS PATTY'S PRINCE

I dragged myself back to the spring-house and dropped in front of the fire. What with worry and no sleep and now this new complication I was dead as yesterday's newspaper. I sat there on the floor with my hands around my knees, thinking what to do next, and as I sat there, the crayon enlargement of father on the spring-house wall began to shake its head from side to side, and then I saw it hold out its hand and point a finger at me.

"Cut and run, Minnie," it said. "Get out from under! Go and buy Timmon's candy store before the smash—the smash—!"

When I opened my eyes Mr. Pierce was sitting on the other side of the chimney and staring at the fire. He had a pipe between his teeth, but he wasn't smoking, and he had something of the same look about his mouth he'd had the first day I saw him.

"Well?" he said, when he saw I was awake.

"I guess I was sleeping." I sat up and pushed in my hairpins and yawned. I was tireder than ever. "I'm clean worn out."

"Of course you're tired," he declared angrily. "You're not a horse, and you haven't been to bed for two nights."

"Care killed the cat," I said. "I don't mind losing sleep, but it's like walking in a swamp, Mr. Pierce. First I put a toe in—that was when I asked you to stay over night. Then I went a step farther, lured on, as you may say, by Miss Patty waving a crown or whatever it is she wants, just beyond my nose. And to-night I've got a—well, to-night I'm in to the neck and yelling for a quick death."

He leaned over to where I sat before the fire and twisted my head toward him.

"To-night—what?" he demanded.

But that minute I made up my mind not to tell him. He might think the situation was too much for him and leave, or he might decide he ought to tell Miss Summers where Dick was. There was no love lost between him and Mr. Carter.

"To-night—I'm just tired and cranky," I said, "so—is Miss Summers settled yet?"

He nodded, as if he wasn't thinking of Miss Summers.

"What did you tell her?"

"Haven't seen her," he said. "Sent her a note that I was understudying a man named Carter and to mind to pick up her cues."

"It's a common enough name," I said, but he had lighted his pipe again and had dropped forward, one elbow on his knee, his hand holding the bowl of his pipe, and staring into the fire. He looked up when I closed and locked the pantry door.

"I've just been thinking," he remarked, "here we are—a group of people—all struggling like mad for one thing, but with different motives. Mine are plain enough and mercenary enough, although a certain red-haired girl with a fine loyalty to an old doctor and a sanatorium is carrying me along with her enthusiasm. And Van Alstyne's motives are clear enough—and selfish. Carter is merely trying to save his own skin—but a girl like Miss Pat—Miss Jennings!"

"There's nothing uncertain about what she wants, or wrong either," I retorted. "She's right enough. The family can't stand a scandal just now with her wedding so close."

He smiled and got up, emptying his pipe.

"Nevertheless, oh, Minnie, of the glowing hair and heart," he said, "Miss Jennings has disappointed me. You see, I believe in marrying for love."

"Love!" I was disgusted. "Don't talk to me about love! Love is the sort of thing that makes two silly idiots run away and get married and live in a shelter-house, upsetting everybody's plans, while their betters have to worry themselves sick and carry them victuals."

He got up and began to walk up and down the spring-house, scowling at the floor.

"Of course," he agreed, "he may be a decent sort, and she may really want him."

"Of course she does!" I said. He stopped short. "I've been wanting a set of red puffs for three years, and I can hardly walk past Mrs. Yost's window down in the village. They've got some that match my hair and I fairly yearn for them. But if I got 'em I dare say I'd put them in a box and go after wanting something else. It's the same way with Miss Patty. She'll get her prince, and because it isn't real love, but only the same as me with the puffs, she'll go after wanting something else. Only she can't put him away in a box. She'll have to put him on and wear him for better, for worse."

"Lord help her!" he said solemnly, and went over to the window and stood there looking out.

I went over beside him. From the window we could see the three rows of yellow lights that marked the house, and somebody with a lantern was going down the path toward the stables. Mr. Pierce leaned forward, his hands at the top of the window-sash, and put his forehead against the glass.

"Why is it that a lighted window in a snow-storm always makes a fellow homesick?" he said in his half-mocking way. "If he hasn't got a home it makes him want one."

"Well, why don't you get one?" I asked.

"On nothing a year?" he said. "Not even prospects! And set up housekeeping in the shelter-house with my good friend Minnie carrying us food and wearing herself to a shadow, not to mention bringing trashy books to my bride."

"She isn't that kind," I broke in, and got red. I'd been thinking of Miss Patty. But he went over to the table and picked up his glass of spring water, only to set it down untasted.

"No, she's not that kind!" he agreed, and never noticed the slip.

"You know, Minnie, women aren't all alike, but they're not all different. An English writer has them classified to a T—there's the mother woman—that's you. You're always mothering somebody with that maternal spirit of yours. It's a pity it's vicarious."

I didn't say anything, not knowing just what he meant. But I've looked it up since and I guess he was about right.

"And there's the mistress woman—Mrs. Dicky, for example, or—" he saw Miss Cobb's curler on the mantel and picked it up—"or even Miss Cobb," he said. "Coquetry and selfishness without maternal instinct. How much of Miss Cobb's virtue is training and environment, Minnie, not to mention lack of temptation, and how much was born in her?"

"She's a preacher's daughter," I remarked. I could understand about Mrs. Dicky, but I thought he was wrong about Miss Cobb.

"Exactly," he said. "And the third kind of woman is the mistress-mother kind, and they're the salt of the earth, Minnie." He began to walk up and down by the spring with his hands in his pockets and a far-away look in his eyes. "The man who marries that kind of woman is headed straight for paradise."

"That's the way!" I snapped. "You men have women divided into classes and catalogued like horses on sale."

"Aren't they on sale?" he demanded, stopping. "Isn't it money, or liberty, or—or a title, usually?" I knew he was thinking of Miss Patty again.

"As for the men," I continued, "I guess you can class the married ones in two classes, providers and non-providers. They're all selfish and they haven't enough virtue to make a fuss about."

"I'd be a shining light in the non-provider class," he said, and picking up his old cap he opened the door. Miss Patty herself was coming up the path.

She was flushed from the cold air and from hurrying, and I don't know that I ever saw her look prettier. When she came into the light we could both see that she was dressed for dinner. Her fur coat was open at the neck, and she had only a lace scarf over her head. She was a disbeliever in colds, anyhow, and all winter long she slept with the windows open and the steam-heat off!

"I'm so glad you're still here, Minnie!" she exclaimed, breathing fast. "You haven't taken the dinner out to the shelter-house yet, have you?"

"Not yet," I replied. "Tillie hasn't brought the basket. The chef's been fussing about the stuff we're using in the diet kitchen the last few days, and I wouldn't be surprised if he's shut off all extras."

But I guess her sister and Mr. Dick could have starved to death just then without her noticing. She was all excitement, for all she's mostly so cool.

"I have a note here for my sister," she said, getting it out of her pocket. "I know we all impose on you, Minnie, but—will you take it for me? I'd go, but I'm in slippers, and, anyhow, I'd need a lantern, and that would be reckless, wouldn't it?"

"In slippers!" Mr. Pierce interrupted. "It's only five degrees above zero! Of all the foolhardy—!"

Miss Patty did not seem to hear him. She gave the letter to me and followed me out on the step.

"You're a saint, Minnie," she said, leaning over and squeezing my arm, "and because you're going back and forth in the cold so much, I want you to have this—to keep."

She stooped and picked up from the snow beside the steps something soft and furry and threw it around my neck, and the next instant I knew she was giving me her chinchilla set, muff and all. I was so pleased I cried, and all the way over to the shelter-house I sniveled and danced with joy at the same time. There's nothing like chinchilla to tone down red hair.

Well, I took the note out to the shelter-house, and rapped. Mr. Dick let me in, and it struck me he wasn't as cheerful as usual. He reached out and took the muff.

"Oh," he said, "I thought that was the supper."

"It's coming," I said, looking past him for Mrs. Dicky. Usually when I went there she was drawing Mr. Dick's profile on a bit of paper or teaching him how to manicure his nails, but that night she was lying on the cot and she didn't look up.

"Sleeping?" I asked in a whisper.

"Grumping!" Mr. Dick answered. He went over and stood looking down at her with his hands in his pockets and his hair ruffled as if he'd been running his fingers through it. She never moved a shoulder.

"Dorothy," he said. "Here's Minnie."

She pretended not to hear.

"Dorothy!" he repeated. "I wish you wouldn't be such a g—Confound it, Dolly, be reasonable. Do you want to make me look like a fool?"

She turned her face enough to uncover one eye.

"It wouldn't be difficult," she answered, staring at him with the one eye. It was red from crying.

"Now listen, Dolly." He got down on one knee beside the cot and tried to take her hand, but she jerked it away. "I've tried wearing my hair that way, and it—it isn't becoming, to say the least. I don't mind having it wet and brushed back in a pompadour, if you insist, but I certainly do balk at the ribbon."

"You've only got to wear the ribbon an hour or so, until it dries." She brought her hand forward an inch or so and he took it and kissed it. It should have been slapped.

"I'll tell you what I'll do," he said. "You can fix it any way you please, when it's too late for old Sam or Pierce to drop in, and I'll wear the confounded ribbon all night. Won't that do?"

But she had seen the note and sat up and held out her hand for it. She was wearing one of Miss Patty's dresses and it hung on her—not that Miss Patty was large, but she had a beautiful figure, and Mrs. Dicky, of course, was still growing and not properly filled out.

"Dick!" she said suddenly, "what do you think? Oskar is here! Pat's in the wildest excitement. He's in town, and Aunt Honoria has telephoned to know what to do! Listen: he is incog., of course, and registered as Oskar von Inwald. He did an awfully clever thing—came in through Canada while the papers thought he was in St. Moritz."

"For heaven's sake," replied Mr. Dick, "tell her not to ask him here. I shouldn't know how to talk to him."

"He speaks lovely English," declared Mrs. Dick, still reading.

"I know all that," he said, walking around nervously, "but if he's going to be my brother-in-law, I suppose I don't get down on my knees and knock my head on the floor. What do I say to him? Your Highness? Oh, I've known a lord or two, but that's different. You call them anything you like and lend them money."

"I dare say you can with Oskar, too." Mrs. Dicky put the note down and sighed. "Well, he's coming. Pat says dad won't go back to town until he's had twenty-one baths, and he's only had eleven and she's got to stay with him. And you needn't worry about what to call Oskar. He's not to know we're here."

I was worried on my way back to the spring-house—not that the prince would make much difference, as far as I could see things being about as bad as they could be. But some of the people were talking of leaving, and since we had to have a prince it seemed a pity he wasn't coming with all his retinue and titles. It would have been a good ten thousand dollars' worth of advertising for the place, and goodness knows we needed it.

When I got back to the spring-house Miss Patty and Mr. Pierce were still there. He was in front of the fire, with his back to it, and she was near the door.

"Of course it isn't my affair," he was saying. "You are perfectly—" Then I opened the door and he stopped. I went on into the pantry to take off my overshoes, and as I closed the door he continued. "I didn't mean to say what I have. I meant to explain about the other night—I had a right to do that. But you forced the issue."

"I was compelled to tell you he was coming," she said angrily. "I felt I should. You have been good enough to take Mr. Carter's place here and save me from an embarrassing situation—"

"I had no philanthropic motives," he insisted stubbornly. "I did it, as you must know, for three meals a day and a roof over my head. If you wish me to be entirely frank, I disapprove of the whole thing."

I heard the swish of her dress as she left the door and went toward him.

"What would you have had me do?" she asked.

"Take those two children to your father. What if there was a row? Why should there be such a lot made of it, anyhow? They're young, but they'll get older. It isn't a crime for two people to—er—love each other, is it? And if you think a scandal or two in your family—granting your father would make a scandal—is going to put another patch on the ragged reputations of the royal family of—"

"How dare you!" she cried furiously. "How DARE you!"

I heard her cross the room and fling the door open and a second later it slammed. When I came out of the pantry Mr. Pierce was sitting in his old position, elbow on knee, holding his pipe and staring at the bowl.

CHAPTER XII

WE GET A DOCTOR

I had my hands full the next day. We'd had another snow-storm during the night and the trains were blocked again. About ten o'clock we got a telegram from the new doctor we'd been expecting, that he'd fallen on the ice on his way to the train and broken his arm, and at eleven a delegation from the guests waited on Mr. Pierce and told him they'd have to have a house physician at once.

Senator Biggs was the spokesman. He said that, personally, he couldn't remain another day without one; that he should be under a physician's care every moment of his fast, and that if no doctor came that day he'd be in favor of all the guests showing their displeasure by leaving together.

"Either that," Thoburn said from the edge of the crowd, "or call it a hotel at once and be done with it. A sanatorium without a doctor is like an omelet without eggs!"

"Hamlet without ham," somebody said.

"We're doing the best we can," Mr. Pierce explained. "We—we expect a doctor to-day."

"When?" from Mr. Jennings, who had come on a cane and was watching Mr. Pierce like a hawk.

"This afternoon, probably. As there is no one here very ill—"

But at that they almost fell on him and tore him to pieces. I had to step in front of him myself and say we'd have somebody there by two o'clock if we had to rob a hospital to get him. And Mr. Sam cried, "Three cheers for Minnie, the beautiful spring-house girl!" and led off.

There's no doubt about it—a man ought to be born to the sanatorium business. A real strong and healthy man has no business trying to run a health resort, and I saw Mr. Pierce wasn't making the hit that I'd expected him to.

He was too healthy. You only needed to look at him to know that he took a cold plunge every morning, and liked to walk ten miles a day, and could digest anything and go to sleep the minute his head touched the pillow. And he had no tact. When Mrs. Biggs went to him and explained that the vacuum cleaner must not be used in her room—that it exhausted the air or something, and she could hardly breathe after it—he only looked bewildered and then drew a diagram to show her it was impossible that it could exhaust the air. The old doctor knew how: he'd have ordered an oxygen tank opened in the room after the cleaner was used and she'd have gone away happy.

Of course Mr. Pierce was most polite. He'd listen to their complaints—and they were always complaining, that's part of the regime—with a puzzled face, trying to understand, but he couldn't. He hadn't a nerve in his body. Once, when one of the dining-room girls dropped a tray of dishes and half the women went to bed with headache from the nervous shock, he never even looked up, but went on with his dinner, and the only comment he made afterward was to tell the head waitress to see that Annie didn't have to pay breakage—that the trays were too heavy for a woman, anyhow. As Miss Cobb said, he was impossible.

Well, as if I didn't have my hands full with getting meals to the shelter-house, and trying to find a house doctor, and wondering how long it would be before "Julia" came face to face with Dick Carter somewhere or other, and trying to keep one eye on Thoburn while I kept Mr. Pierce straight with the other—that day, during luncheon, Mike the bath man came out to the spring-house and made a howl about his wages. He'd been looking surly for two days.

"What about your wages?" I snapped. "Aren't you getting what you've always had?"

"No tips!" he said sulkily. "Only a few taking baths—only one daily, and that's that man Jennings. There's no use talking, Miss Minnie, I've got to have a double percentage on that man or you'll have to muzzle him. He—he's dangerous."

"If I give you the double percentage, will you stay?"

"I don't know but that I'd rather have the muzzle, Miss Minnie," he answered slowly, "but—I'll stay. It won't be for long."

Which left me thinking. I'd seen Thoburn talking to Mike more than once lately, and he'd been going around with an air of assurance that didn't make me any too cheerful. Evenings, when I'd relieved Amanda King at the news stand, I'd seen Thoburn examining the woodwork of the windows, and only the night before, happening on the veranda unexpectedly, I found Mike and him measuring it with a tape line. As I say, Mike's visit left me thinking.

The usual crowd came out that afternoon and drank water and sat around the fire and complained—all except Senator Biggs, who happened in just as I was pouring melted butter over a dish of hot salted pop-corn. He stood just inside the door, sniffling, with his eyes fixed on the butter, and then groaned and went out.

He looked terrible—his clothes hung on him like bags; as the bishop said, it was ghastly to see a convexity change to such a concavity in three days.

Mr. Moody won three dollars that day from the slot-machine and was almost civil to his wife, but old Jennings sat with his foot on a stool and yelled if anybody slammed the door. Mrs. Hutchins brought him out with her eyes red and asked me if she could leave him there.

"I'm sorry if I was rude to you the other night, Minnie," she said, "but I was upset. I'm so worn-out that I'll have to lie down for an hour, and if he doesn't get better soon, I—I shall have to have help. My nerves are gone."

At four o'clock Mr. Sam came in, and he had Mr. Thoburn tight by the arm.

"My dear old chap," he was saying, "it would be as much as your life's worth. That ground is full of holes and just now covered with snow—!"

He caught my eye, and wiped his forehead.

"Heaven help us!" he said, coming over to the spring, "I found him making for the shelter-house, armed with a foot rule! Somebody's got to take him in hand—I tell you, the man's a menace!"

"What about the doctor?" I asked, reaching up his glass.

"Be here to-night," he answered, "on the—"

But at that minute a boy brought a telegram down and handed it to him. The new doctor was laid up with influenza!

We sat there after the others had gone, and Mr. Sam said he was for giving up the fight, only to come out now with the truth would mean such a lot of explaining and a good many people would likely find it funny. Mr. Pierce came in later and we gave him the telegram to read.

"I don't see why on earth they need a doctor, anyhow," he said, "they're not sick. If they'd take a little exercise and get some air in their lungs—"

"My dear fellow," Mr. Sam cried in despair, "some people are born in sanatoriums, some acquire them, and others have them thrust upon them—I've had this place thrust upon me. I don't know why they want a doctor, but they do. They balked at Rodgers from the village. They want somebody here at night. Mr. Jennings has the gout and there's the deuce to pay. Some of them talk of leaving."

"Let 'em leave," said Mr. Pierce. "If they'd go home and drink three gallons of any kind of pure water a day—"

"Sh! That's heresy here! My dear fellow, we've got to keep them."

Mr. Pierce glanced at the telegram and handed it back.

"Lot's of starving M. D.'s would jump at the chance," he said, "but if it's as urgent as all this we can't wait to hunt. I'll tell you, Van Alstyne, there's a chap down in the village he was the character man with the Sweet Peas Company—and he's stranded there. I saw him this morning. He's washing dishes in the depot restaurant for his meals. We used to call him Doc, and I've a hazy idea that he's a graduate M. D.—name's Barnes."

"Great!" cried Mr. Van Alstyne. "Let's have Barnes. You get him, will you, Pierce?"

Mr. Pierce promised and they started out together. At the door Mr. Sam turned.

"Oh, by the way, Minnie," he called, "better gild one of your chairs and put a red cushion on it. The prince has arrived."

Well, I thought it all out that afternoon as I washed the glasses, and it was terrible. I had two people in the shelter-house to feed and look after like babies, with Tillie getting more curious every day about the basket she brought, and not to be held much longer; and I had a man running the sanatorium and running it to the devil as fast as it could go. Not that he wasn't a nice young man, big, strong-jawed and all that, but you can't make a diplomat out of an ordinary man in three days, and it takes more diplomacy to run a sanatorium a week than it does to be secretary of state for four years. Then I had a prince incognito, and Thoburn stirring up mischief, and the servants threatening to strike, and no house doctor—

Just as I got to that somebody opened the door behind me and looked in. I glanced around, and it was a man with the reddest hair I ever saw. Mine was pale by comparison. He was rather short and heavy-set, and he had a pleasant face, although not handsome, his nose being slightly bent to the left. But at first all I could see was his hair.

"Good evening," he said, edging himself in. "Are you Miss Waters?"

"Yes," I said, rising and getting a glass ready, "although I'm not called that often, except by people who want to pun on my name and my business." I looked at him sharply, but he hadn't intended any pun.

He took off his hat and came over to the spring where I was filling his glass.

"If that's for me, you needn't bother," he said. "If it tastes as it smells, I'm not thirsty. My name's Barnes, and I was to wait here for Mr. Van Alstyne."

"Barnes!" I repeated. "Then you're the doctor."

He grinned, and stood turning his hat around in his hands.

"Not exactly," he said. "I graduated in medicine a good many years ago, but after a year of it, wearing out more seats of trousers waiting for patients than I earned enough to pay for, and having to have new trousers, I took to other things."

"Oh, yes," I said. "You're an actor now."

He looked thoughtful.

"Some people think I'm not," he answered, "but I'm on the stage. Graduated there from prize-fighting. Prize-fighting, the stage, and then writing for magazines—that's the usual progression. Sometimes, as a sort of denouement before the final curtain, we have dinner at the White House."

I took a liking to the man at once. It was a relief to have somebody who was willing to tell all about himself and wasn't incognito, or in hiding, or under somebody else's name. I put a fresh log on the fire, and as it blazed up I saw him looking at me.

"Ye gods and little fishes!" he said. "Another redhead! Why, we're as alike as two carrots off the same bunch!"

In five minutes I knew how old he was, and where he was raised, and that what he wanted more than anything on earth was a little farmhouse with chickens and a cow.

"Where you can have air, you know," he said, waving his hands, which were covered with reddish hair. "Lord, in the city I starve for air! And where, when you're getting soft you can go out and tackle the wood-pile. That's living!"

And then he wanted to know what he was to do at the sanatorium and I told him as well as I could. I didn't tell him everything, but I explained why Mr. Pierce was calling himself Carter, and about the two in the shelter-house. I had to. He knew as well as I did that three days before Mr. Pierce had had nothing to his name but a folding automobile road map or whatever it was.

"Good for old Pierce!" he said when I finished. "He's a prince, Miss Waters. If you'd seen him sending those girls back to town—well, I'll do all I can to help him. But I'm not much of a doctor. It's safe to acknowledge it; you'll find it out soon enough."

Mr. and Mrs. Van Alstyne came in just then, and Mr. Sam told him what he was expected to do. It wasn't much: he was to tell them at what temperatures to take their baths, "and Minnie will help you out with that," he added, and what they were to eat and were not to eat. "Minnie will tell you that, too," he finished, and Mr. Barnes, DOCTOR Barnes, came over and shook my hand.

"I'm perfectly willing to be first assistant," he declared. "We'll put our heads together and the result will be—"

"Combustion!" said Mr. Sam, and we all laughed.

"Remember," Mr. Sam instructed him, as Doctor Barnes started out, "when you don't know what to prescribe, order a Turkish bath. The baths are to a sanatorium what the bar is to a club—they pay the bills."

Well, we got it all fixed and Doctor Barnes started out, but at the door he stopped.

"I say," he asked in an undertone, "the stork doesn't light around here, does he?"

"Not if they see him first!" I replied grimly, and he went out.

CHAPTER XIII

THE PRINCE—PRINCIPALLY

It was all well enough for me to say—as I had to to Tillie many a time—that it was ridiculous to make a fuss over a person for what, after all, was an accident of birth. It was well enough for me to say that it was only by chance that I wasn't strutting about with a crown on my head and a man blowing a trumpet to let folks know I was coming, and by the same token and the same chance Prince Oskar might have been a red-haired spring-house girl, breaking the steels in her figure stooping over to ladle mineral water out of a hole in the earth.

Nevertheless, at five o'clock, after every one had gone, when I saw Miss Patty, muffled in furs, tripping out through the snow, with a tall thin man beside her, walking very straight and taking one step to her four, I felt as though somebody had hit me at the end of my breast-bone.

They stopped a minute outside before they came in, and I had to take myself in hand.

"Now look here, Minnie, you idiot," I said to myself, "this is America; you're as good as he is; not a bend of the knee or a stoop of the neck. And if he calls you 'my good girl' hit him."

They came in together, laughing and talking, and, to be honest, if I hadn't caught the back of a chair, I'd have had one foot back of the other and been making a courtesy in spite of myself.

"We're late, Minnie!" Miss Patty said. "Oskar, this is one of my best friends, and you are to be very nice to her."

He had one of those single glass things in his eye and he gave me a good stare through it. Seen close he was handsomer than Mr. Pierce, but he looked older than his picture.

"Ask her if she won't be nice to me," he said in as good English as mine, and held out his hand.

"Any of Miss Patty's friends—" I began, with a lump in my throat, and gave his hand a good squeeze. I thought he looked startled, and suddenly I had a sort of chill.

"Good gracious!" I exclaimed, "should I have kissed it?"

They roared at that, and Miss Patty had to sit down in a chair.

"You see, she knows, Oskar," she said. "The rest are thinking and perhaps guessing, but Minnie is the only one that knows, and she never talks. Everybody who comes here tells Minnie his troubles."

"But—am I a trouble?" he asked in a low tone. I was down in the spring, but I heard it.

"So far you have hardly been an unalloyed joy," she replied, and from the spring I echoed "Amen."

"Yes—I'm so hung with family skeletons that I clatter when I walk," I explained, pretending I hadn't heard, and brought them both glasses of water. "It's got to be a habit with some people to save their sciatica and their husband's dispositions and their torpid livers and their unpaid bills and bring 'em here to me."

He sniffed at the glass and put it down.

"Herr Gott!" he said, "what a water! It is—the whole thing is extraordinary! I can understand the reason for Carlsbad or Wiesbaden—it is gay. One sees one's friends; it is—social. But here—!"

He got up and, lifting a window curtain, peered out into the snow.

"Here," he repeated, "shut in by forests and hills, a thousand miles from life—" He shrugged his shoulders and came back to the table. "It is well enough for the father," he went on to Miss Patty, "but for you! Why—it is depressing, gray. The only bit of color in it all is—here, in what you call the spring-house." I thought he meant Miss Patty's cheeks or her lovely violet eyes, but he was looking at my hair. I had caught his eye on it before, but this time he made no secret about it, and he sighed, for all the world as if it reminded him of something. He went over to the slot-machine and stood in front of it, humming and trying the different combinations. I must say he had a nice back.

Miss Patty came over and slipped her hand in mine.

"Well?" she whispered, looking at me with her pretty eyebrows raised.

"He looks all right," I had to confess. "Perhaps you can coax him to shave."

She laughed.

"Oskar!" she called, "you have passed, but you are conditioned. Minnie objects to the mustache."

He turned and looked at me gravely.

"It is my—greatest attraction," he declared, "but it is also a great care. If Miss Minnie demands it, I shall give it to her in a—in a little box." He sauntered over and looked at me in his audacious way. "But you must promise to care for it. Many women have loved it."

"I believe that!" I answered, and stared back at him without blinking. "I guess I wouldn't want the responsibility."

But I had an idea that he meant what he said about the many women, and that Miss Patty knew it as well as I did. She flushed a little, and they went very soon after that. I stood and watched them until they disappeared in the snow, and I felt lonelier than ever, and sad, although certainly he was better than I had expected to find him. He was a man, and not a little cub with a body hardly big enough to carry his forefathers' weaknesses. But he had a cold eye and a warm mouth, and that sort of man is generally a social success and a matrimonial failure.

It wasn't until toward night that I remembered I'd been talking to a real prince and I hadn't once said "your Highness" or "your Excellency" or whatever I should have said. I had said "You!"

I had hardly closed the door after them when it opened again and Mr. Pierce came in. He shut the door and, going over to one of the tables, put a package down on it.

"Here's the stuff you wanted for the spring, Minnie," he announced. "I suppose I can't do anything more than register a protest against it?"

"You needn't bother doing that," I answered, "unless it makes you feel better. Your authority ends at that door. Inside the spring-house I'm in control."

It's hard to believe, with things as they are, that I once really believed that. But I did. It was three full days later that I learned that I'd been mistaken!

Well, he sat there and looked at nothing while I heated water in my brass kettle over the fire and dissolved the things against Thoburn's quick eye the next day, and he didn't say anything. He had a gift for keeping quiet, Mr. Pierce had. It got on my nerves after a while.

"Things are doing better," I remarked, stirring up my mixture.

"Yes," he said, without moving.

"I suppose they're happier now they have a doctor?"

"Yes—no—I don't know. He's not much of a doctor, you know—and there don't seem to be any medical books around."

"There's one on the care and feeding of infants in the circulating library," I said, "and he can have my Anatomy."

"You're generous!" he remarked, with one of his quick smiles.

"It's a book," I snapped, and fell to stirring again. But he was moping once more, with his feet out and his hands behind his head, staring at the ceiling.

"I say, Minnie—"

"Yes?"

"Miss—Miss Jennings and the von Inwald were here just now, weren't they? I passed them on the bridge."

"Yes."

"What—how do you like him?"

"Better than I expected and not so well as I might," I said. "If you are going to the house soon you might take Miss Patty her handkerchief. It's there under that table."

I took my mixture into the pantry and left it to cool. But as I started back I stopped. He had got the handkerchief and was standing in front of the fire, holding it in the palm of his hand and looking at it. And all in a minute he crushed it to his face with both hands and against the firelight I could see him quivering.

I stepped back into the pantry and came out again noisily. He was standing very calm and quiet where he had been before, and no handkerchief in sight.

"Well," I said, "did you get it?"

"Get what?"

"Miss Patty's handkerchief?"

"Oh—that! Yes. Here it is." He pulled it out of his pocket and held it up by the corner.

"Ridiculous size, isn't it, and—" he held it up to his nose—"I dare say one could almost tell it was hers by the scent. It's—it's like her."

"Humph!" I said, suddenly suspicious, and looked at it. "Well," I said, "it may remind you of Miss Patty, and the scent may be like Miss Patty, but she doesn't use perfume on her handkerchief. This has an E. C. on it, which means Eliza Cobb."

He left soon after, rather crestfallen, but to save my life I couldn't forget what I'd seen—him with that scrap of linen that he thought was hers crushed to his face, and his shoulders heaving. I had an idea that he hadn't cared much for women before, and that, this being a first attack, he hadn't established what the old doctor used to call an immunity.

CHAPTER XIV

PIERCE DISAPPROVES

Mrs. Hutchins came out to the spring-house the next morning. She was dressed in a black silk with real lace collar and cuffs, and she was so puffed up with pride that she forgot to be nasty to me.

"I thought I'd better come to you, Minnie," she said. "There seems to be nobody in authority here any more. Mr. Carter has put the—has put Mr. von Inwald in the north wing. I can not imagine why he should have given him the coldest and most disagreeable part of the house."

I said I'd speak to Mr. Carter and try to have him moved, and she rustled over to where I was brushing the hearth and stooped down.

"Mr. von Inwald is incognito, of course," she said, "but he belongs to a very old family in his own country—a noble family. He ought to have the best there is in the house."

I promised that, too, and she went away, but I made up my mind to talk to Mr. Pierce. The sanatorium business isn't one where you can put your own likes and dislikes against the comfort of the guests.

Miss Cobb came out a few minutes after; she had on her new green silk with the white lace trimming. She saw me staring as she threw off her cape and put her curler on the log.

"It's a little dressy for so early, of course, Minnie," she said, "but I wish you'd see some of the other women! Breakfast looked like an afternoon reception. What would you think of pinning this black velvet ribbon around my head?"

"It might have done twenty years ago, Miss Cobb," I answered, "but I wouldn't advise it now." I was working at the slot-machine, and I heard her sniff behind me as she hung up her mirror on the window-frame.

She tried the curler on the curtain, which she knows I object to, but she was too full of her subject to be sulky for long.

"I wish you could see Blanche Moody!" she began again, standing holding the curler, with a thin wreath of smoke making a halo over her head. "Drawn in—my dear, I don't see how she can breathe! I guess there's no doubt about Mr. von Inwald."

"I'd like to know who put this beer check in the slot-machine yesterday," I said as indifferently as I could. "What about Mr. von Inwald?"

She tiptoed over to me, the halo trailing after her.

"About his being a messenger from the prince to Miss Jennings!" she answered in a whisper. "He spent last night closeted with papa, and the chambermaid on that floor told Lily Biggs that there was almost a quarrel."

"That doesn't mean anything," I objected. "If the Angel Gabriel was shut in with Mr. Jennings for ten minutes he'd be blowing his trumpet for help."

Miss Cobb shrugged her shoulders and took hold of a fresh wisp of hair with the curler.

"I dare say," she assented, "but the Angel Gabriel wouldn't have waited to breakfast with Miss Jennings, and have kissed her hand before everybody at the foot of the stairs!"

"Is he handsome?" I asked, curious to know how he would impress other women. But Miss Cobb had never seen a man she would call ugly.

"Handsome!" she said. "My dear, he's beautiful! He has a duel scar on his left cheek—all the nobility have them over there. I've a cousin living in Berlin—she's the wittiest person—and she says the German child of the future will be born with a scarred left cheek!"

Well, I was sick enough of hearing of Mr. von Inwald before the day was over. All morning in the spring-house they talked Mr. von Inwald. They pretended to play cards, but they were really playing European royalty. Every time somebody laid down a queen, he'd say, "Is the queen still living, or didn't she die a few years ago?" And when they played the knave, they'd start off about the prince again. They'd all decided that Mr. von Inwald was noble—somebody said that the "von" was a sort of title. The women were planning to make the evenings more cheerful, too. They couldn't have a dance with the men using canes or forbidden to exercise, but Miss Cobb had a lot of what she called "parlor games" that she wanted to try out. "Introducing the Jones family" was one of them.

In the afternoon Mr. von Inwald came out to the spring-house and sat around, very affable and friendly, drinking the water. He and the bishop grew quite chummy. Miss Patty was not there, but about four o'clock Mr. Pierce came out. He did not sit down, but wandered around the room, not talking to anybody, but staring, whenever he could, at the prince. Once I caught Mr. von Inwald's eyes fixed on him, as if he might have seen him before. After a while Mr. Pierce sat down in a corner like a sulky child and filled his pipe, and as nobody noticed him except to complain about the pipe, which he didn't even hear, he sat there for a half-hour, bent forward, with his pipe clenched in his teeth, and never took his eyes off Mr. von Inwald's face.

Senator Biggs was the one who really caused the trouble. He spent a good deal of time in the spring-house trying to fool his stomach by keeping it filled up all the time with water. He had got past the cranky stage, being too weak for it; his face was folded up in wrinkles like an accordion and his double chin was so flabby you could have tucked it away inside his collar.

"What do you think of American women, Mr. von Inwald?" he asked, and everybody stopped playing cards and listened for the answer. As Mr. von Inwald represented the prince, wouldn't he be likely to voice the prince's opinion of American women?

It's my belief Mr. von Inwald was going to say something nice. He smiled as if he meant to, but just then he saw Mr. Pierce in his corner sneering behind his pipe. They looked at each other steadily, and nobody could mistake the hate in Mr. Pierce's face or his sneer. After a minute the prince looked away and shrugged his shoulders, but he didn't make his pretty speech.

"American women!" he said, turning his glass of spring water around on the table before him, "they are very lovely, of course." He looked around and there were Mrs. Moody and Mrs. Biggs and Miss Cobb, and he even glanced at me in the spring. Then he looked again at Mr. Pierce and kept his eyes there. "But they are spoiled, fearfully spoiled. They rule their parents and they expect to rule their husbands. In Europe we do things better; we are not—what is the English?—hag-ridden?"

There was a sort of murmur among the men, but the women all nodded as if they thought Europe was entirely right. They'd have agreed with him if he'd advocated sixteen wives sitting cross-legged on a mat, like the Turks. Mr. Pierce was still staring at the prince.

"What I don't quite understand, Mr. von Inwald," the bishop put in in his nice way, "is your custom of expecting a girl to bring her husband a certain definite sum of money and to place it under the husband's control. Our wealthy American girls control their own money," He was thinking of Miss Patty, and everybody knew it.

The prince turned red and glared at the bishop. Then I think he remembered that they didn't know who he was, and he smiled and started to turning the glass again.

"Pardon!" he said. "Is it not better? What do women know of money? They throw it away on trifles, dress, jewels—American women are extravagant. It is one result of their—of their spoiling."

Mr. Pierce got up and emptied his pipe into the fire. Then he turned.

"I'm afraid you have not known the best type of American women," he said, looking hard at the prince. "Our representative women are our middle-class women. They do not contract European alliances, not having sufficient money to attract the attention of the nobility, or enough to buy titles, as they do pearls, for the purpose of adornment."

Mr. von Inwald got up, and his face was red. Mr. Pierce was white and sneering.

"Also," he went on, "when they marry they wish to control their own money, and not see it spent in—ways with which you are doubtless familiar."

We were all paralyzed. Nobody moved. Mr. Pierce put his pipe in his pocket and stalked out, slamming the door. Then Mr. von Inwald shrugged his shoulders and laughed.

"I see I shall have to talk to our young friend," he said and picked up his glass. "I'm afraid I've given a wrong impression. I like the American women very much; too well," he went on with a flash of his teeth, looking around the room, and brought the glass to the spring for me to fill. But as I've said before, I can tell a good bit about a man from the way he gives me his glass, and he was in a perfect frenzy of rage. When I reached it back to him he gripped it until his nails were white.

My joint ached all the rest of the afternoon. About five o'clock Mr. Thoburn stopped in long enough to say: "What's this I hear about Carter making an ass of himself to-day?"

"I haven't heard it," I answered. "What is it?"

But he only laughed and turned up his collar to go.

"Jove, Minnie," he said, "why do women of your spirit always champion the losing side? Be a good girl; give me a hand now and then with this thing, and I'll see you don't lose by it."

"We're not going to lose," I retorted angrily. "Nobody has left yet. We are still ahead on the books."

He came over and shook a finger in my face.

"Nobody has left—and why? Because they're all taking a series of baths. Wait until they've had their fifteen, or twenty-one, or whatever the cure is, and then see them run!"

It was true enough; I knew it.

CHAPTER XV

THE PRINCE, WITH APOLOGIES

Tillie brought the supper basket for the shelter-house about six o'clock and sat down for a minute by the fire. She said Mr. Pierce Carter to her had started out with a gun about five o'clock. It was foolish, but it made me uneasy.

"They've gone plumb crazy over that Mr. von Inwald," she declared. "It makes me tired. How do they know he's anything but what he says he is? He may be a messenger from the emperor of Austria, and he may be selling flannel chest protectors. Miss Cobb's all set up; she's talking about getting up an entertainment and asking that Miss Summers to recite."

She got up, leaving the basket on the hearth.

"And say," she said, "you ought to see that dog now. It's been soakin' in peroxide all day!"

She went out with the peroxide, but a moment later she opened the door and stuck her head in, nodding toward the basket.

"Say," she said, "the chef's getting fussy about the stuff I'm using in the diet kitchen. You've got to cut it out soon, Minnie. If I was you I'd let him starve."

"What!" I screeched, and grasped the rail of the spring.

"Let him starve!" she repeated.

"Wha—what are you talking about?" I demanded when I got my voice.

She winked at me from the doorway.

"Oh, I'm on all right, Minnie!" she assured me, "although heaven only knows where he puts it all! He's sagged in like a chair with broken springs."

I saw then that she thought I was feeding Senator Biggs on the sly, and I breathed again. But my nerves were nearly gone, and when just then I heard a shot from the direction of the deer park, even Tillie noticed how pale I got.

"I don't know what's come over you, Minnie," she said. "That's only Mr. Carter shooting rabbits. I saw him go out as I started down the path."

I was still nervous when I put on my shawl and picked up the basket. But there was a puddle on the floor and the soup had spilled. There was nothing for it but to go back for more soup, and I got it from the kitchen without the chef seeing me. When I opened the spring-house door again Mr. Pierce was by the fire, and in front of him, where I'd left the basket, lay a dead rabbit. He was sitting there with his chin in his hands looking at the poor thing, and there was no basket in sight.

"Well," I asked, "did you change my basket into a dead rabbit?"

"Basket!" he said, looking up. "What basket?"

I looked everywhere, but the basket was gone, and after a while I decided that Mr. Dick had had an attack of thoughtfulness or hunger and had carried it out himself.

And all the time I looked for the basket Mr. Pierce sat with the gun across his knees and stared at the rabbit.

"I'd thank you to take that messy thing out of here," I told him.

"Poor little chap!" he exclaimed. "He was playing in the snow, and I killed him—not because I wanted food or sport, Minnie, but—well, because I had to kill something."

"I hope you don't have those attacks often," I said. He looked at the rabbit and sighed.

"Never in my life!" he answered. "For food or sport, that's different, but—blood-lust!" He got up and put the gun in the corner, and I saw he looked white and miserable.

"I don't like myself to-night, Minnie," he said, trying to smile, "and nobody likes me. I'm going into the garden to eat worms!"

I didn't like to scold him when he was feeling bad anyhow, but business is business. So I asked him how long he thought people would stay if he acted as he had that day. I said that a sanatorium was a place where the man who runs it can't afford to have likes and dislikes; that for my part I'd a good deal rather he'd get rid of his excitement by shooting off a gun, provided he pointed it away from the house, than to sit around and let his mind explode and kill all our prospects. I told him, too, to remember that he wasn't responsible for the morals or actions of his guests, only for their health.

"Health!" he echoed, and kicked a chair. "Health! Why, if I wanted to keep a good dog in condition, Minnie, I wouldn't bring him here."

"No," I retorted, "you'd shut him in an old out oven, and give him a shoe to chew, and he'd come out in three days frisking and happy. But you can't do that with people."

"Why not?" he asked. "Although, of course, the supply of out ovens and old shoes is limited here."

"As far as Mr. von Inwald goes," I went on, "that's not your affair or mine. If Miss Patty's own father can't prevent it, why should you worry about it?"

"Precisely," he agreed. "Why should I? But I do, Minnie—that's the devil of it."

"There are plenty of nice girls," I suggested, feeling rather sorry for him.

"Are there? Oh, I dare say." He stooped and picked up his rabbit. "Straight through the head; not so bad for twilight. Poor little chap!"

He said good night and went out, taking the gun and the rabbit with him, and I went into the pantry to finish straightening things for the night. In a few minutes I heard voices in the other room, one Mr. Pierce's, and one with a strong German accent.

"When was that?" Mr. von Inwald's voice.

"A year ago, in Vienna."

"Where?"

"At the Bal Tabarin. You were in a loge. The man I was with told me who the woman was. It was she, I think, who suggested that you lean over the rail—"

"Ah, so!" said Mr. von Inwald as if he just remembered. "Ah, yes, I recall—I was with—the lady was red-haired, is it not? And it was she who desired me—"

"You leaned over the rail and poured a glass of wine on my head. It was very funny. The lady was charmed."

"I recall it perfectly. I remember that I did it under protest—it was a very fine wine, and expensive."

"Then you also recall," said Mr. Pierce, very quietly, "that because you were with a—well, because you were with a woman, I could not return your compliment. But I demanded the privilege at some future date when you were alone."

"It is a pity," replied Mr. von Inwald, "that now, when I am alone, there is no wine!"

"No, there is no wine," Mr. Pierce agreed slowly, "but there is—"

I opened the door at that, and both of them started. Mr. von Inwald was standing with his arms folded, and Mr. Pierce had one arm raised holding up a glass of spring water. In another second it would have been in the other man's face.

I walked over to Mr. Pierce and took the glass out of his hand, and his expression was funny to see.

"I've been looking everywhere for that glass," I said. "It's got to be washed."

Mr. von Inwald laughed and picked up his soft hat from the table.

He turned around at the door and looked back at Mr. Pierce, still laughing.

"Accept my apologies!" he said. "It was such a fine wine, and so expensive."

Then he went out.

CHAPTER XVI

STOP, THIEF!

I was pretty nervous when I took charge of the news stand that evening. Amanda King had an appointment with the dentist and had left everything topsyturvey. I was still straightening up when people began to come down to dinner.

Miss Cobb walked over to the news stand, and she'd cut the white yoke out of her purple silk. She looked very dressy, although somewhat thin.

"Everybody has dressed for dinner to-night, Minnie," she informed me. "We didn't want Mr. von Inwald to have a wrong idea of American society, especially after Mr. Carter's ridiculous conduct this afternoon, and I wonder if you'll be sweet enough to start the phonograph in the orchestra gallery as we go in—something with dignity, you know—the wedding march, or the overture from Aida."

"Aida's cracked," I said shortly, "and as far as I'm concerned, Mr. von Inwald can walk in to his meals without music, or starve to death waiting for the band."

But she got the phonograph, anyhow, and put the elevator boy in the gallery with it. She picked out some things by Caruso and Tetrazzini and piled them on a chair, but James had things to himself up there, and played The Spring Chicken through three times during dinner, with Miss Cobb glaring at the gallery until the back of her neck ached, and the dining-room girls waltzing in with the dishes and polka-ing out.

Mr. Moody came out when dinner was over in a fearful rage and made for the news stand.

"One of your ideas, I suppose," he asserted. "What sort of a night am I going to have after chewing my food to rag-time, with my jaws doing a skirt-dance? Why in heaven's name couldn't you have had something slow, like Handel's Largo, if you've got to have music?"

But dinner was over fifteen minutes sooner than usual. James cake-walked everybody out to My Ann Elizer, and Miss Cobb was mortified to death.

Two or three things happened that night. For one, I got a good look at Miss Julia Summers. She was light-haired and well-fleshed, with an ugly face but a pleasant smile. She wore a low-necked dress that made Miss Cobb's with the yoke out look like a storm collar, and if she had a broken heart she didn't show it.

"Hello," she cried, looking at my hair, "are you selling tobacco here or are you the cigar-lighter?"

"Neither," I answered, looking over her head. "I am employed as the extinguisher of gay guests."

"Good," she said, smiling. "I'm something fine at that myself. Suppose I stay here and help. If I watch that line of knitting women I'll be crotcheting Arabella's wool in my sleep to-night."

Well, she was too cheerful to be angry with. So she stayed around for a while, and it was amazing how much tobacco I sold that evening. Men who usually bought tobies bought the best cigars, and when Mr. Jennings came up, scowling, and I handed him the brand he'd smoked for years, she took one, clipped the end of it as neat as a finger nail and gave it to him, holding up the lighter.

"I'm not going to smoke yet, young woman," he said, glaring at her. But she only smiled.

"I'm sorry," she said. "I've been waiting hungrily until some discriminating smoker would buy one of those and light it. I love the aroma."

And he stood there for thirty minutes, standing mostly on one foot on account of the gouty one, puffing like a locomotive, with her sniffing at the aroma and telling him how lonely she felt with no friends around and just recovering from a severe illness.

At eight o'clock he had Mrs. Hutchins bring him his fur-lined coat and he and Miss Julia took Arabella, the dog, for a walk on the veranda!

The rest of the evening was quiet, and I needed it. Miss Patty and Mr. von Inwald talked by the fire and I think he told her something—not all—of the scene in the spring-house. For she passed Mr. Pierce at the foot of the stairs on her way up for the night and she pretended not to see him. He stood there looking up after her with his mouth set, and at the turn she glanced down and caught his eye. I thought she flushed, but I wasn't sure, and at that minute Senator Biggs bought three twenty-five-cent cigars and told me to keep the change from a dollar. I was so surprised at the alteration in him that I forgot Miss Patty entirely.

About twelve o'clock, just after I went to my room, somebody knocked at the door. When I opened, the new doctor was standing in the hall.

"I'm sorry to disturb you," he said, "but nobody seems to know where the pharmacy clerk is and I'll have to get some medicine."

"If I'd had my way, we'd have had a bell on that pharmacy clerk long ago," I snapped, getting my keys. "Who's sick?"

"The big man," he replied. "Biggs is his name, I think, a senator or something."

I was leading the way to the stairs, but I stopped. "I might have known it," I said. "He hasn't been natural all evening. What's the matter with him? Too much fast?"

"Fast!" He laughed. "Too much feast! He's got as pretty a case of indigestion as I've seen for some time. He's giving a demonstration that's almost theatrical."

Well, he insisted it was indigestion, although I argued that it wasn't possible, and he wanted ipecac.

"I haven't seen a pharmacopoeia for so long that I wouldn't know one if I met it," he declared, "but I've got a system of mnemonics that never fails. Ipecac and colic both end with 'c'—I'll never forget that conjunction. It was pounded in and poured in in my early youth."

Well, the pharmacy was locked, and we couldn't find a key to fit it. And when I suggested mustard and warm water he jumped at the idea.

"Fine!" he said. "Better let me dish out the spring-water and you take my job! Lead on, MacDuff, to the kitchen."

Although it was only midnight there was not a soul about. A hall leads back of the office to the kitchen and pantries, and there was a low light there, but the rest was dark. We bumped through the diet kitchen and into the scullery, when we found we had no matches. I went back for some, and when I got as far as the diet kitchen again Doctor Barnes was there, just inside the door.

"Sh!" he whispered. "Come into the scullery. The kitchen is dark, but there is somebody in there, fumbling around, striking matches. I suppose you don't have such things as burglars in this neck of the woods?"

Well, somebody had broken into Timmons' candy store a week before and stolen a box of chewing-gum and a hundred post-cards, and I told him so in a whisper.

"Anyhow, it isn't the chef," I said. "He's had a row with the bath man and is in bed with a cut hand and a black eye, and nobody else has any business here."

We tiptoed into the scullery in the dark: just then somebody knocked a kettle down in the kitchen and it hit the stove below with a crash. Whoever was there swore, and it was not Francois, who expresses his feelings mostly in French. This was English.

There's a little window from the kitchen into the scullery as well as a door. The window had a wooden slide and it was open an inch or so. We couldn't see anything, but we could hear a man moving around. Once he struck a match, but it went out and he said "Damn!" again, and began to feel his way toward the scullery.

Doctor Barnes happened to touch my hand and he patted it as if to tell me not to be frightened. Then he crept toward the scullery door and waited there.

It swung open slowly, but he waited until it closed again and the man was in the room. Then he yelled and jumped and there was the sound of a fall. I could hardly strike the match—I was trembling so—but when I did there was Mr. Dick lying flat on the floor and the doctor sitting on him.

"Mister Dick!" I gasped, and dropped the match.

"Something hit me!" Mr. Dick said feebly, and when I had got a candle lighted and had explained to Doctor Barnes that it was a mistake, he got off him and let him up. He was as bewildered as Mr. Dick and pretty nearly as mad.

We put him—Mr. Dick—in a chair and gave him a glass of water, and after he had got his breath—the doctor being a heavy man—he said he was trying to find something to eat.

"Confound it, Minnie," he exclaimed, "we're starving! It seems to me there are enough of you here at least to see that we are fed. Not a bite since lunch!"

"But I thought you had the basket," I explained. "I left it at the spring-house, and when I went back it was gone."

"So that was it!" he answered. And then he explained that just about the time they expected their supper they saw a man carry a basket stealthily through the snow to the deer park. It was twilight, but they watched him from the window, and he put the basket through the barbed-wire fence and then crawled after it. Just inside he sat down on a log and, opening the basket, began to eat. He was still there when it got too dark to see him.

"If that was our dinner," he finished savagely, "I hope he choked to death over it."

Doctor Barnes chuckled. "He didn't," he said, "but he's got the worst case of indigestion in seven counties."

Well, I got the mustard and water ready with Mr. Dick standing by hoping Mr. Biggs would die before he got it, and then I filled a basket for the shelter-house. I put out the light and he took the basket and started out, but he came back in a hurry.

"There's somebody outside talking," he said. I went to the door with him and listened.

"The sooner the better," Mike was saying. "I'm no good while I've got it on my mind."

And Mr. Thoburn: "To-morrow is too soon: they're not in the mood yet. Perhaps the day after. I'll let you know."

I didn't get to sleep until almost morning, and then it was to dream that Mr. Pierce was shouting "Hypocrites" to all the people in the sanatorium and threatening to throw glasses of mustard and warm water at them.

CHAPTER XVII

A BUNCH OF LETTERS

When people went down to breakfast the next morning they found a card hanging on the office door with a half dozen new rules on it, and when I went out to the spring-house the guests were having an indignation meeting in the sun parlor, with the bishop in the chair, and Senator Biggs, so wobbly he could hardly stand, making a speech.

I tried to see Mr. Pierce, but early as it was he had gone for a walk, taking Arabella with him. So I called a conference at the shelter-house—Miss Patty, Mr. and Mrs. Van Alstyne, Mr. and Mrs. Dick, and myself. Mrs. Dick wasn't dressed, but she sat up on the edge of her cot in her dressing-gown, with her feet on the soap box, and yawned. As we didn't have enough chairs, Miss Patty jerked the soap box away and made me sit down. Mr. Dick was getting breakfast.

We were in a tight place and we knew it.

"He is making it as hard for us as he can," Mrs. Sam declared. "The idea of having the card-room lights put out at midnight, and the breakfast room closed at ten! Nobody gets up at that hour."

"He was to come here every evening for orders," said Mr. Dick, measuring ground coffee with a tablespoon, as I had showed him. "He came just once, and as for orders—well, he gave 'em to me!"

But Miss Patty was always fair.

"I loathe him," she asserted. "I want to quarrel with him the minute I see him. He—he is presumptuous to the point of impertinence—but he's honest: he thinks we're all hypocrites—those that are well and those that are sick or think they are—and he hates hypocrisy."

Everybody talked at once, then, and she listened.

"Very well," she said. "I'll amend it. We're not all hypocrites. My motives in all this are perfectly clear—and selfish."

"You and old Pierce would make a fine team, Pat," Mrs. Dick remarked with a yawn. "I like hypocrites myself. They're so comfy. But if you're not above advice, Pat, you'll have Aunt Honoria break her neck or something—anything to get father back to town. Something is going to explode, and Oskar doesn't like to be agitated."

She curled up on the cot with that and went sound asleep. The rest of us had coffee and talked, but there wasn't anything to do. As Mr. Sam said, Mr. Pierce didn't want to stay, anyhow, and as likely as not if we went to him in a body and told him he must come to the shelter-house for instructions, and be suave and gentle when he was called down by the guests about the steam-pipes making a racket, he'd probably prefer to go down to the village and take Doctor Barnes' place washing dishes at the station. That wouldn't call for any particular mildness.

But he settled it by appearing himself. He came across the snow from the direction of Mount Hope, and he had a pair of skees over his shoulder. At that time I didn't even know the name of the things, but I learned enough about them later. I must say he looked very well beside Mr. Dick, who wasn't very large, anyhow, and who hadn't had time to put on his collar, and Mr. Sam, who's always thin and sallow and never takes a step he doesn't have to.

I let him in, and when he saw us all there he started and hesitated.

"Come in, Pierce," Mr. Sam said. "We've just been talking about you."

He came in, but he didn't look very comfortable.

"What have you decided to do with me?" he asked. "Put me under restraint?"

He was unbuttoning his sweater, and now he took out two of the smallest rabbits I ever saw and held them up by the ears. Miss Patty gave a little cry and took them, cuddling them in her lap.

"They're starving and almost frozen, poor little devils," he said. "I found them near where I shot the mother last night, Minnie, and by way of atonement I'm going to adopt them."

Well, although the minute before they'd all been wishing they'd never seen him, they pretty nearly ate him up. Miss Patty held the rabbits, so we all had turns at feeding them warm milk with a teaspoon and patting their pink noses. When it came Mr. Pierce's turn they were about full up, so he curled his big body on the floor at Miss Patty's feet and talked to the rabbits and looked at her. He had one of those faces that's got every emotion marked on it as clear as a barometer—when he was mad his face was mad all over, and when he was pleased he glowed to the tips of his ears. And he was pleased that morning.

But, of course, he had to be set right about the sanatorium, and Mr. Sam began it. Mr. Pierce listened, sitting on the floor and looking puzzled and more and more unhappy. Finally he got up and drew a long breath.

"Exactly," he agreed. "I know you are all right and I'm wrong—according to your way of thinking. But if these people want to be well, why should I encourage them to do the wrong thing? They eat too much, they don't exercise"—he turned to Mr. Van Alstyne.

"Why, do you know, I asked a half dozen of the men—one after the other—to go skeeing with me this morning and not one of them accepted!"

"Really!" Mr. Sam exclaimed mockingly.

"What can you do with people like that?" Mr. Pierce went on. "They don't want to be well; they're all hypocrites. Look at that man Biggs! I'll lay you ten to one that after fasting five days and then stealing a whole chicken, a dozen oysters and Lord knows what else, now that he's sick, he'll hold it against me."

"He's not holding anything," I objected.

"Because HE is a hypocrite—" Mr. Sam began.

"That's not the point, Pierce," Mr. Dick broke in importantly. "You were to come here for orders and you haven't done it. You're running this place for me, not for yourself."

Mr. Pierce looked at Mr. Dick and from there to Mr. Sam and smiled.

"I did come," he explained. "I came twice, and each time we played roulette. I lost all the money I'd had in advance. Honestly," he confessed, "I felt I couldn't afford to come every day."

Miss Patty got up and put the baby rabbits into her sister's big fur muff.

"We are all talking around the question," she said. "Mr. Pierce undertook to manage the sanatorium, and to try to manage it successfully. He can not do that without making some attempt at conciliating the people. It's—it's absurd to antagonize them."

"Exactly," he said coldly. "I was to manage it, and to try to do it successfully. I'm sorry my methods don't meet with the approval of this—er—executive committee. But it might as well be clear that I intend to use my own methods—or none."

Well, what could we do? Miss Patty went out with her head up, and the rest of us stayed and ate humble pie, and after a while he agreed to stay if he wasn't interfered with. He said he and Doctor Barnes had a plan that he thought was a winner—that it would either make or break the place, and he thought it would make it. And by that time we were so meek that we didn't even ask what it was.

Doctor Barnes and Miss Summers were the first to come to the mineral spring that morning. She stopped just inside the door and sniffed.

"Something's dead under the floor," she said.

"If there's anything dead," Doctor Barnes replied, "it's in the center of the earth. That's the sulphur water."

She came in at that, but unwillingly, and sat down with her handkerchief to her nose. Then she saw me.

"Good gracious!" she exclaimed. "What have you done that they put you here?"

"If you mean the bouquet from the spring, you get to like it after a while," I said grimly. "Ordinary air hasn't got any snap for me now."

"Humph!" She looked at me suspiciously, but I was busy wiping off the tables. "Well," she said, holding up the glass Doctor Barnes had brought her, "it doesn't cost me anything, so here goes. But think of paying money for it!"

She drank it down in a gulp and settled herself in her chair.

"What'll it do to me?" she asked. "Mixed drinks always play the deuce with me, Barnes, and you know it."

"If you'll cut down your diet and take some exercise it will make you thin," I began. "'The process is painless and certain: kindly nature in her benevolent plan—'"

"Give me another!" she interrupted, and Doctor Barnes filled her glass again. "Some women spell fate f-a-t-e," she said, looking at the water, "but I spell it without the e."

She took half of it and then put down the glass. "Honestly," she declared, "I'd rather be fat."

Mr. Pierce met them there a few minutes later and they had a three-cornered chat. But Miss Summers evidently didn't know just how much I knew and was careful of what she said. Once, however, when I was in the pantry she thought I was beyond ear-shot.

"Good heavens, Pierce," she said, "if they could put THAT in a play!"

"Cut it out, Julia," Doctor Barnes snapped, and it wasn't until they had gone that I knew she'd meant me. I looked through the crack of the door and she was leaning over taking a puff at Doctor Barnes' cigarette.

"Curious old world, isn't it?" she said between puffs. "Here we are the three of us—snug and nice, having seven kinds of hell-fire water and not having to pay for it; three meals a day and afternoon tea ditto, good beds and steam-heat ditto—and four days ago where were we? Pierce, you were hocking your clothes! Doc, you—"

"Washing dishes!" he said. "I never knew before how extravagant it is to have a saucer under a cup!"

"And I!" she went on, "I, Julia Summers, was staring at a ceiling in the Finleyville hotel, with a face that looked like a toy balloon."

"And now," said Doctor Barnes, "you are more beautiful than ever. I am a successful physician—oh, lord, Julia, if you'd hear me faking lines in my part! And my young friend here—Pierce—Julia, Pierce has now become a young reprobate named Dicky Carter, and may the Lord have mercy on his soul!"

I tried to get out in time, but I was too late. I saw her rise, saw the glass of water at her elbow roll over and smash on the floor, and saw her clutch wildly at Mr. Pierce's shoulder.

"Not—not DICKY Carter!" she cried.

"Richard—they call him Dick," Mr. Pierce said uneasily, and loosened her fingers from his coat.

Oh, well, everybody knows it now—how she called Mr. Dick everything in the calendar, and then began to cry and said nobody would ever know what she'd been through with, and the very dress she had on was a part of the trousseau she'd had made, and what with the dressmaker's bills—

Suddenly she stopped crying.

"Where is he, anyhow?" she demanded.

"All we are sure of," Mr. Pierce replied quietly, "is that he is not in the sanatorium."

She looked at us all closely, but she got nothing from my face.

"Oh, very well," she said, shrugging her shoulders, "I'll wait until he shows up. It doesn't cost anything."

Then, with one of her easy changes, she laughed and picked up her muff to go.

"Minnie and I," she said, "will tend bar here, and in our leisure moments we will pour sulphur water on a bunch of Dicky's letters that I have, to cool 'em." She walked to the door and turned around, smiling.

"Carry fire insurance on 'em all the time," she finished and went out, leaving us staring at one another!

CHAPTER XVIII

MISS COBB'S BURGLAR

I went to bed early that night. What with worrying and being alternately chilled by tramping through the snow and roasted as if I was sitting on a volcano with an eruption due, I was about all in. We'd been obliged to tell Mrs. Sam about the Summers woman, and I had to put hot flannels on her from nine to ten. She was quieter when I left her, but, as I told Mr. Sam, it was the stillness of despair, not resignation.

I guess it was about four o'clock in the morning when a hand slid over my face, and I sat up and yelled. The hand covered my mouth at that, and something long and white and very thin beside the bed said: "Sh! For heaven's sake, Minnie!"

It was Miss Cobb! It was lucky I came to my senses when I did, for her knees gave way under her just then and she doubled up on the floor beside the bed with her face in my comfort.

I lighted a candle and set it on a chair beside the bed and took a good look at her. She was shaking all over, which wasn't strange, for I sleep with my window open, and she had a key in her hand.

"Here," she gasped, holding out the key, "here, Minnie, wake the house and get him, but, oh, Minnie, for heaven's sake, save my reputation!"

"Get who?" I demanded, for I saw it was her room key.

"I have been coming here for ten years," she groaned, out of the comfort, "and now, to be bandied about by the cold breath of scandal!"

I shook her by the shoulder

"The cold breath you are raving about is four degrees below zero. If you can't tell me what's the matter I'm going back to bed and cover my feet."

She got up at that and stood swaying, with her nightgown flapping around her like a tent.

"I have locked a man in my room!" she declared in a terrible voice, and collapsed into the middle of the bed.

Well, I leaned over and tried to tell her she'd made a mistake. The more I looked at her, with her hair standing straight out over her head, and her cambric nightgown with a high collar and long sleeves, and the hump on her nose where her brother Willie had hit her in childhood with a baseball bat, the surer I was that somebody had made a mistake—likely the man.

Now there's two ways to handle a situation like that: one of them is to rouse the house—and many a good sanatorium has been hurt by a scandal and killed by a divorce; the other way is to take one strong man who can hold his tongue, find the guilty person, and send him a fake telegram the next morning that his mother is sick. I've done that more than once.

I sat down on the side of the bed and put on my slippers.

"What did he look like?" I asked. "Could you see him?"

She uncovered one eye.

"Not—not distinctly," she said. "I—think he was large, and—and rather handsome. That beast of a dog must have got in my room and was asleep under the bed, for it wakened me by snarling."

There was nothing in that to make me nervous, but it did. As I put on my kimono I was thinking pretty hard.

I could not waken Mr. Pierce by knocking, so I went in and shook him. He was sound asleep, with his arms over his head, and when I caught his shoulder he just took my hand and, turning over, tucked it under his cheek and went asleep again.

"Mr. Pierce! Mr. Pierce!" He wakened a little at that, but not enough to open his eyes. He seemed to know that the hand wasn't his, however, for he kissed it. And with that I slapped him and he wakened. He lay there blinking at my candle and then he yawned.

"Musht have been ashleep!" he said, and turned over on his other side and shut his eyes.

It was two or three minutes at least before I had him sitting on the side of the bed, with a blanket spread over his knees, and was telling him about Miss Cobb.

"Miss Cobb!" he said. "Oh, heavens, Minnie, tell her to go back to bed!" He yawned. "If there's anybody there it's a mistake. I'm sleepy. What time is it?"

"I'm not going out of this room until you get up!" I declared grimly.

"Oh, very well!" he said, and put his feet back into bed. "If you think I'm going to get up while you're here—"

After he seemed pretty well wakened I went out. I waited in the sitting-room and I heard him growling as he put on his clothes. When he came out, however, he was more cheerful, and he stopped in the hall to fish a case out of Mr. Sam's dressing-gown pocket and light a cigarette.

"Now!" he said, taking my arm. "Forward, the light-ly clad brigade! But—" he stopped—"Minnie, we are unarmed! Shall I get the patent folding corkscrew?"

He had to be quiet when we got to the bedroom floors, however, and when we stopped outside Miss Cobb's door he was as sober as any one could wish him.

"You needn't come in," he whispered. "Ten to one she dreamed it, but if she didn't you're better outside. And whatever you hear, don't yell."

I gave him the key and he fitted it quietly in the lock. Arabella, just inside, must have heard, for she snarled. But the snarl turned into a yelp, as if she'd been suddenly kicked.

Mr. Pierce, with his hand on the knob, turned and looked at me in the candle-light. Then he opened the door.

Arabella gave another yelp and rushed out; she went between my feet like a shot and almost overthrew me, and when I'd got my balance again I looked into the room. Mr. Pierce was at the window, staring out, and the room was empty.

"The idiot!" Mr. Pierce said. "If it hadn't been for that snowbank! Here, give me that candle!"

He stood there waving it in circles, but there was neither sight nor sound from below. After a minute Mr. Pierce put the window down and we stared at the room. All the bureau drawers were out on the floor, and the lid of poor Miss Cobb's trunk was open and the tray upset. But her silver-backed brush was still on the bureau and the ring the insurance agent had given her lay beside it.

We brought her back to her room, and she didn't know whether to be happy that she was vindicated or mad at the state her things were in. I tucked her up in bed after she'd gone over her belongings and Mr. Pierce had double-locked the window and gone out. She drew my head down to her and her eyes were fairly popping out of her head.

"I feel as though I'm going crazy, Minnie!" she whispered, "but the only things that are gone are my letters from Mr. Jones, and—my black woolen tights!"

CHAPTER XIX

NO MARRIAGE IN HEAVEN

I slept late the next morning, and when I'd had breakfast and waded to the spring-house it was nearly nine. It was still snowing, and no papers or mail had got through, although the wires were still in fair working order.

As I floundered out I thought I saw somebody slink around the corner of the spring-house, but when I got there nobody was in sight. I was on my knees in front of the fireplace, raking out the fire, when I heard the door close behind me, and when I turned, there stood Mr. Dick, muffled to the neck, with his hat almost over his face.

"What the deuce kept you so late this morning?" he demanded, in a sulky voice, and limping over to a table he drew a package out of his pocket and slammed it on the table.

"I was up half the night, as usual," I said, rising. "You oughtn't to be here, Mr. Dick!"

He caught hold of the rail around the spring, and hobbling about, dropped into a chair with a groan.

"For two cents," he declared, "I'd chop a hole in the ice pond and drown myself. There's no marriage in Heaven."

"That's no argument for the other place," I answered, and stopped, staring. He was pulling something out of his overcoat pocket, an inch at a time.

"For God's sake, Minnie," he exclaimed, "return this—this garment to—whomever it belongs to!"

He handed it to me, and it was Miss Cobb's black tights! I stood and stared.

"And then," he went on, reaching for the package on the table, "when you've done that, return to 'Binkie' these letters from her Jonesie."

He took the newspaper off the bundle then, and I saw it was wrapped with a lavender ribbon. I sat down and gazed at him, fascinated. He was the saddest-eyed piece of remorse I'd seen for a long time.

"And when you've got your breath back, Minnie," he said feebly, "and your strength, would you mind taking the floor mop and hitting me a few cracks? Only not on the right leg, Minnie—not on the right leg. I landed on it last night; it's twisted like a pretzel."

"Don't stand and stare," he continued irritably, when I didn't make a move, "at least get that—that infernal black garment out of sight. Cover it with the newspaper. And if you don't believe that a sweet-faced young girl like my wife has a positive talent for wickedness and suspicion, go out to the shelter-house this morning."

"So it was you!" I gasped, putting the newspaper over the tights.

"Why in the name of peace did you jump out the window, and what did you want with—with these things?"

He twisted around in his chair to stare at me, and then stooped and clutched frantically at his leg, as if for inspiration.

"Want with those things!" he snarled. "I suppose you can't understand that a man might wake up in the middle of the night with a mad craving for a pair of black woolen tights, and—"

"You needn't be sarcastic with me," I broke in. "You can save that for your wife. I suppose you also had a wild longing for the love-letters of an insurance agent—"

And then it dawned on me, and I sat down and laughed until I cried.

"And you thought you were stealing your own letters!" I cried. "The ones she carries fire insurance on! Oh, Mr. Dick, Mr. Dick!"

"How was I to know it wasn't Ju—Miss Summers' room?" he demanded angrily. "Didn't I follow the dratted dog? And wouldn't you have thought the wretched beast would have known me instead of sitting on its tail under the bed and yelling for mother? I gave her the dog myself. Oh, I tell you, Minnie, if I ever get away from this place—"

"You've got to get away this minute," I broke in, remembering. "They'll be coming any instant now."

He got up and looked around him helplessly.

"Where'll I go?" he asked. "I can't go back to the shelter-house."

I looked at him and he tried to grin.

"Fact," he said, "hard to believe, but—fact, Minnie. She's got the door locked. Didn't I tell you she is of a suspicious nature? She was asleep when I left, and mostly she sleeps all night. And just because she wakes when I'm out, and lets me come in thinking she's asleep, when she has one eye open all the time, and she sees what I'd never even seen myself—that the string of that damned garment, whatever it is, is fastened to the hook of my shoe, me thinking all the time that the weight was because I'd broken my leg jumping—doesn't she suddenly sit up and ask me where I've been? And I—I'm unsuspicious, Minnie, by nature, and I said I'd been asleep. Then she jumped up and showed me that—that thing— those things, hanging to my shoe, and she hasn't spoken to me since. I wish I was dead."

And just then a dog barked outside and somebody on the step stamped the snow off his feet. We were both paralyzed for a moment.

"Julia!" Mr. Dick cried, and went white.

I made a leap for the door, just as the handle turned, and put my back against it.

"Just a minute," I called. "The carpet is caught under it!"

Mr. Dick had lost his head and was making for the spring, as if he thought hiding his feet would conceal him. I made frantic gestures to him to go into my pantry, and he went at last, leaving his hat on the table, I left the door and flung it after him—the hat, of course, not the door—and when Miss Summers sauntered in just after, I was on my knees brushing the hearth, with my heart going three-four time and skipping every sixth beat.

"Hello!" she said. "Lovely weather—for polar bears. If the natives wade through this all winter it's no wonder they walk as if they are ham-strung. Don't bother getting me a glass. I'll get my own."

She was making for the pantry when I caught her, and I guess I looked pretty wild.

"I'll get it," I said. "I—that's one of the rules."

She put her hands in the pockets of her white sweater and smiled at me.

"Do you know," she declared, "the old ladies' knitting society isn't so far wrong about you! About your making rules—whatever you want, WHENEVER you want 'em."

She put her head on one side.

"Now," she went on, "suppose I break that rule and get my own glass? What happens to me? I don't think I'll be put out!"

I threw up my hands in despair, for I was about at the end of my string.

"Get it then!" I exclaimed, and sat down, waiting for the volcano to erupt. But she only laughed and sat down on a table, swinging her feet.

"When you know me better, Minnie," she said, "you'll know I don't spoil sport. I happen to know you have somebody in the pantry—moreover, I know it's a man. There are tracks on the little porch, my dear girl, not made by your galoshes. Also, my dearest girl, there's a gentleman's glove by your chair there!" I put my foot on it. "And just to show you what a good fellow I am—"

She got off the table, still smiling, and sauntered to the pantry door, watching me over her shoulder.

"Don't be alarmed!" she called through the door, "I'm not coming in! I shall take my little drink of nature's benevolent remedy out of the tin ladle, and then—I shall take my departure!"

My heart was skipping every second beat by that time, and Miss Julia stood by the pantry door, her head back and her eyes almost closed, enjoying every minute of it. If Arabella hadn't made a diversion just then I think I'd have fainted.

She'd pulled the newspaper and the tights off the table and was running around the room with them, one leg in her mouth.

"Stop it, Arabella!" said Miss Julia, and took the tights from her. "Yours?" she asked, with her eyebrows raised.

"No—yes," I answered.

"I'd never have suspected you of them!" she remarked. "Hardly sheer enough to pull through a finger ring, are they?" She held them up and gazed at them meditatively. "That's one thing I draw the line at. On the boards, you know—never have worn 'em and never will. They're not modest, to my mind,—and, anyhow, I'm too fat!"

Mr. Sam and his wife came in at that moment, Mr. Sam carrying a bottle of wine for the shelter-house, wrapped in a paper, and two cans of something or other. He was too busy trying to make the bottle look like something else—which a good many people have tried and failed at—to notice what Miss Summers was doing, and she had Miss Cobb's protectors stuffed in her muff and was standing very dignified in front of the fire by the time they'd shaken off the snow.

"Good morning!" she said.

"Morning!" said Mr. Sam, hanging up his overcoat with one hand, and trying to put the bottle in one of the pockets with the other. Mrs. Sam didn't look at her.

"Good morning, Mrs. Van Alstyne!" Miss Summers almost threw it at her. "I spoke to you before; I guess you didn't hear me."

"Oh, yes, I heard you," answered Mrs. Sam, and turned her back on her. Give me a little light-haired woman for sheer devilishness!

I'd expected to see Miss Summers fly to pieces with rage, but she stared at Mrs. Sam's back, and after a minute she laughed.

"I see!" she remarked slowly. "You're the sister, aren't you?"

Mr. Sam had given up trying to hide the bottle and now he set it on the floor with a thump and came over to the fire.

"It's—you see, the situation is embarrassing," he began. "If we had had any idea—"

"I might have been still in the Finleyville hotel!" she finished for him. "Awful thought, isn't it?"

"Under the circumstances," went on Mr. Sam, nervously, "don't you think it would be—er—better form if er—under the circumstances—"

"I'm thinking of my circumstances," she put in, good-naturedly. "If you imagine that six weeks of one-night stands has left me anything but a rural wardrobe and a box of dog biscuit for Arabella, you're pretty well mistaken. I haven't even a decent costume. All we had left after the sheriff got through was some grass mats, a checked sunbonnet and a pump."

"Minnie," Mrs. Sam said coldly, "that little beast of a dog is trying to drink out of the spring!"

I caught her in time and gave her a good slapping. When I looked up Miss Summers was glaring down at me over the rail.

"Just what do you mean by hitting my dog?" she demanded. It was the first time I'd seen her angry.

"Just what I appeared to mean," I answered. "If you want to take it as a love pat, you may." And I stalked to the door and threw the creature out into the snow. It was the first false step that day; if I'd known what putting that dog out meant—! "I don't allow dogs here," I said, and shut the door.

Miss Summers was furious; she turned and stared at Mrs. Sam, who was smiling at the fire.

"Let Arabella in," she said to me in an undertone, "or I'll open the pantry door!"

"Open the door!" I retorted. I was half hysterical, but it was no time to weaken. She looked me straight in the eye for fully ten seconds; then, to my surprise, she winked at me. But when she turned on Mr. Sam she was cold rage again and nothing else.

"I am not going to leave, if that is what you are about to suggest," she said. "I've been trying to see Dicky Carter the last ten days, and I'll stay here until I see him."

"It's a delicate situation—"

"Delicate!" she snapped. "It's indelicate it's indecent, that's what it is. Didn't I get my clothes, and weren't we to have been married by the Reverend Dwight Johnstone, out in Salem, Ohio? And didn't he go out there and have old Johnstone marry him to somebody else? The wretch! If I ever see him—"

A glass dropped in the pantry and smashed, but nobody paid any attention.

"Oh, I'm not going until he comes!" she continued. "I'll stay right here, and I'll have what's coming to me or I'll know the reason why. Don't forget for a minute that I know why Mr. Pierce is here, and that I can spoil the little game by calling the extra ace, if I want to."

"You're forgetting one thing," Mrs. Sam said, facing her for the first time, "if you call the game, my brother is worth exactly what clothes he happens to be wearing at the moment and nothing else. He hasn't a penny of his own."

"I don't believe it," she sniffed. "Look at the things he gave me!"

"Yes. I've already had the bills," said Mr. Sam.

She whirled and looked at him, and then she threw back her head and laughed.

"You!" she said. "Why, bless my soul! All the expense of a double life and none of its advantages!"

She went out on that, still laughing, leaving Mrs. Sam scarlet with rage, and when she was safely gone I brought Mr. Dick out to the fire. He was so limp he could hardly walk, and it took three glasses of the wine and all Mr. Sam could do to start him back to the shelter-house. His sister would not speak to him.

Mike went to Mr. Pierce that day and asked for a raise of salary.

He did not get it. Perhaps, as things have turned out, it was for the best, but it is strange to think how different things would have been if he'd been given it. He was sent up later, of course, for six months for malicious mischief, but by that time the damage was done.

CHAPTER XX

EVERY DOG HAS HIS DAY

That was on a Saturday morning. During the golf season Saturday is always a busy day with us, with the husbands coming up for over Sunday, and trying to get in all the golf, baths and spring water they can in forty-eight hours. But in the winter Saturday is the same as any, other day.

It had stopped snowing and the sun was shining, although it was so cold that the snow blew like powder. By eleven o'clock every one who could walk had come to the spring-house. Even Mr. Jennings came down in a wheeled chair, and Senator Biggs, still looking a sort of grass-green and keeping his eyes off me, came and sat in a corner, with a book called Fast versus Feast held so that every one could see.

There were bridge tables going, and five hundred, and a group around the slot-machine, while the crocheters formed a crowd by themselves, exchanging gossip and new stitches.

About twelve o'clock Mr. Thoburn came in, and as he opened the door, in leaped Arabella. The women made a fuss over the creature and cuddled her, and when I tried to put her out everybody objected. So she stayed, and Miss Summers put her through a lot of tricks, while the men crowded around. As I said before, Miss Summers was a first favorite with the men.

Mr. von Inwald and Miss Patty came in just then and stood watching.

"And now," said Mr. von Inwald, "I propose, as a reward to Miss Arabella, a glass of this wonderful water. Minnie, a glass of water for Arabella!"

"She doesn't drink out of one of my glasses," I declared angrily.

"It's one of my rules that dogs—"

"Tut!" said Mr. Thoburn. "What's good for man is good for beast. Besides, the little beggar's thirsty."

Well, they made a great fuss about the creature's being thirsty, and so finally I got a panful of spring water and it drank until I thought it would burst. I'm not vicious, as I say, but I wish it had.

Well, the dog finished and lay down by the fire, and everything seemed to go on as before. Mr. Thoburn was in a good humor, and he came over to the spring and brought a trayful of glasses.

"To save you steps, Minnie!" he explained. "You have no idea how it pains me to see you working. Gentlemen, name your poison!"

"A frappe with blotting-paper on the side," Mr. Moody snarled from the slot-machine. "If I drink much more, I'll have to be hooped up like a barrel."

"Just what is the record here?" the bishop asked. "I'm ordered eight glasses, but I find it more than a sufficiency."

"We had one man here once who could drink twenty-five at a time," I said, "but he was a German."

"He was a tank," Mr. Sam corrected grumpily. He was watching something on the floor—I couldn't see what. "All I need is to swallow a few goldfish and I'd be a first-class aquarium."

"What I think we should do," Miss Cobb said, "is to try to find out just what suits us, and stick to that. I'm always trying."

"Damned trying!" Mr. Jennings snarled, and limped over for more water. "I'd like to know where to go for rheumatism."

"I got mine here," said Mr. Thoburn cheerfully. "It's my opinion this place is rheumatic as well as malarious. And as for this water, with all due respect to the spirit in the spring"—he bowed to me—"I think it's an insult to ask people to drink it. It isn't half so strong as it was two years ago. Taste it; smell it! I ask the old friends of the sanatorium, is that water what it used to be?"

"Don't tell me it was ever any worse than this!" Miss Summers exclaimed. But Thoburn went on. The card-players stopped to listen, but Mr. Sam was still staring at something on the floor.

"I tell you, the spring is losing its virtue, and, like a woman, without virtue, it is worthless."

"But interesting!" Mr. Sam said, and stooped down.

"Consider," went on Mr. Thoburn, standing and holding his glass to the light, "how we are at the mercy of this little spring! A convulsion in the bowels of the earth, and its health-giving properties may be changed to the direst poison. How do we know, you and I, some such change has not occurred overnight? Unlikely as it is, it's a possibility that, sitting here calmly, we may be sipping our death potion."

Some of the people actually put down their glasses and everybody began to look uneasy except Mr. Sam, who was still watching something I could not see.

Mr. Thoburn looked around and saw he'd made an impression. "We may," he continued, "although my personal opinion of this water is that it's growing too weak to be wicked. I prove my faith in Mother Nature; if it is poisoned, I am gone. I drink!"

Mr. Sam suddenly straightened up and glanced at Miss Summers. "Perhaps I'm mistaken," he said, "but I think there is something the matter with Arabella."

Everybody looked: Arabella was lying on her back, jerking and twitching and foaming at the mouth.

"She's been poisoned!" Miss Summers screeched, and fell on her knees beside her. "It's that wretched water!"

There was pretty nearly a riot in a minute. Everybody jumped up and stared at the dog, and everybody remembered the water he or she had just had, and coming on top of Mr. Thoburn's speech, it made them babbling lunatics. As I look back, I have a sort of picture of Miss Summers on the floor with Arabella in her lap, and the rest telling how much of the water they had had and crowding around Mr. Thoburn.

"It seems hardly likely it was the water," he said, "although from what I recall of my chemistry it is distinctly possible. Springs have been known to change their character, and the coincidence—the dog and the water—is certainly startling. Still, as nobody feels ill—"

But they weren't sure they didn't. The bishop said he felt perfectly well, but he had a strange inclination to yawn all the time, and Mrs. Biggs' left arm had gone to sleep. And then, with the excitement and all, Miss Cobb took a violent pain in the back of her neck and didn't know whether to cry or to laugh.

Well, I did what I could. The worst of it was, I wasn't sure it wasn't the water. I thought possibly Mr. Pierce had made a mistake in what he had bought at the drug store, and although I don't as a rule drink it myself, I began to feel queer in the pit of my stomach.

Mr. Thoburn came over to the spring, and filling a glass, took it to the light, with every one watching anxiously. When he brought it back he stooped over the railing and whispered to me.

"When did you fix it?" he asked sternly.

"Last night," I answered. It was no time to beat about the bush.

"It's yellower than usual," he said. "I'm inclined to think something has gone wrong at the drug store, Minnie."

I could hardly breathe. I had the most terrible vision of all the guests lying around like Arabella, twitching and foaming, and me going to prison as a wholesale murderess. Any hair but mine would have turned gray in that minute.

Mr. von Inwald was watching like the others, and now he came over and caught Mr. Thoburn by the arm.

"What do you think—" he asked nervously. "I—I have had three glasses of it!"

"Three!" shouted Senator Biggs, coming forward. "I've had eleven! I tell you, I've been feeling queer for twenty-four hours! I'm poisoned! That's what I am."

He staggered out, with Mrs. Biggs just behind him, and from that moment they were all demoralized. I stood by the spring and sipped at the water to show I wasn't afraid of it, with my knees shaking under me and Arabella lying stock-still, as if she had died, under my very nose. One by one they left to look for Doctor Barnes, or to get the white of egg, which somebody had suggested as an antidote.

Miss Cobb was one of the last to go. She turned in the doorway and looked back at me, with tears in her eyes.

"It isn't your fault, Minnie," she said, "and forgive me if I have ever said anything unkind to you." Then she went, and I was alone, looking down at Arabella.

Or rather, I thought I was alone, for there was a movement by one of the windows and Miss Patty came forward and knelt by the dog.

"Of all the absurdities!" she said. "Poor little thing! Minnie, I believe she's breathing!"

She put the dog's head in her lap, and the little beast opened its eyes and tried to wag its blue tail.

"Oh, Miss Patty, Miss Patty!" I exclaimed, and I got down beside her and cried on her shoulder, with her stroking my hand and calling me dearest! Me!

I was wiping my eyes when the door was thrown open and Mr. Pierce ran in. He had no hat on and his hair was powdered with snow. He stopped just inside the door and looked at Miss Patty.

"You—" he said "you are all right? You are not—" he came forward and stood over her, with his heart in his eyes. She MUST have known from that minute.

"My God!" he exclaimed, "I thought you were poisoned!"

She looked up, without smiling, and then I thought she half shut her eyes, as if what she saw in his face hurt her.

"I am all right," she assured him, "and little Arabella will be all right, too. She's had a convulsion, that's all—probably from overeating. As for the others—!"

"Where is the—where is von Inwald?"

"He has gone to take the white of an egg," she replied rather haughtily. She was too honest to evade anything, but she flushed. Of course, I knew what he didn't—that the prince had been among the first to scurry to the house, and that he hadn't even waited for her.

He walked to the window, as if he didn't want her to see what he thought of that, and I saw him looking hard at something outside in the snow. When he walked back to the fire he was smiling, and he stooped over and poked Arabella with his finger.

"So that was it!" he said. "Full to the scuppers, poor little wretch! Minnie, I am hoist with my own petard, which in this case was a boomerang."

"Which is in English—" I asked.

"With the instinct of her sex, Arabella has unearthed what was meant to be buried forever. She had gorged herself into a convulsion on that rabbit I shot last night!"

CHAPTER XXI

THE MUTINY

They went to the house together, he carrying Arabella like a sick baby and Miss Patty beside him. As far as I could see they didn't speak a word to each other, but once or twice I saw her turn and look up at him as if she was puzzled.

I closed the door and stood just inside, looking at father's picture over the mantel. As sure as I stood there, the eyes were fixed on the spring, and I sensed, as you may say, what they meant. I went over and looked down into the spring, and it seemed to me it was darker than usual. It may have smelled stronger, but the edge had been taken off my nose, so to speak, by being there so long.

From the spring I looked again at father, and his eyes were on me mournful and sad. I felt as though, if he'd been there, father would have turned the whole affair to the advantage of the house, and it was almost more than I could bear. I was only glad the old doctor's enlargement had not come yet. I couldn't have endured having it see what had occurred.

The only thing I could think of was to empty the spring and let the water come in plain. I could put a little sulphur in to give it color and flavor, and if it turned out that Mr. Pierce was right and that Arabella was only a glutton, I could put in the other things later.

I was carrying out my first pailful when Doctor Barnes came down the path and took the pail out of my hand.

"What are you doing?" he asked. "Making a slide?"

"No," I said bitterly, "I am watering the flowers."

"Good!" He was not a bit put out. "Let me help you." He took the pail across the path and poured a little into the snow at the base of a half-dozen fence posts. "There!" he said, coming back triumphant. "The roses are done. Now let's have a go at the pansies and the lady's-slippers and the—the begonias. I say"—he stopped suddenly on his way in—"sulphur water on a begonia—what would it make? Skunk cabbage?"

Inside, however, he put down the pail, and pulling me in, closed the door.

"Now forget it!" he commanded. "Just because a lot of damn fools see a dog in a fit and have one, too, is that any reason for your being scared wall-eyed and knock-kneed?"

"I'm not!" I snapped.

"Well, you're wall-eyed with fright," he insisted. "Of course, you're the best judge of your own knees, but after last night—Had any lunch?"

I shook my head.

"Exactly," he said. "You make me think of the little boy who dug post-holes in the daytime and took in washings at night to support the family. Sit down."

I sat.

"Inhale and exhale slowly four times, and then swallow the lump in your throat.... Gone?"

"Yes."

"Good." He was fumbling in his pocket and he brought out a napkin. When he opened it there was a sandwich, a piece of cheese and a banana.

"What do you think of that?" he asked, watching me anxiously. "Looks pretty good?"

"Fine," I said, hating to disappoint him, although I never eat sardines, and bananas give me indigestion, "I'm hungry enough to eat a raw Italian."

"Then fall to," he directed, and with a flourish he drew a bottle of ginger ale from his pocket.

"How's this?" he demanded, holding it up. "Cheers but doesn't inebriate; not a headache in a barrel; ginger ale to the gingery! 'A quart of ale is a dish for a king,'" he said, holding up a glass. "That's Shakespeare, Miss Minnie."

I was a good bit more cheerful when I'd choked down the sandwich, especially when he assured me the water was all right—"a little high, as you might say, but not poisonous. Lord, I wish you could have seen them staggering into my office!"

"I saw enough," I said with a shiver.

"That German, von Inwald," he went on, "he's the limit. He accused us of poisoning him for reasons of state!"

"Where are they now?"

"My dear girl," he answered, putting down his glass, "what has been pounded into me ever since I struck the place? The baths! I prescribe 'em all day and dream 'em all night. Where are the poisonees now? They are steaming, stewing, exuding in the hot rooms of the bath department—all of them, every one of them! In the hold and the hatches down!"

He picked up the pail and went down the steps to the spring.

"After all," he said, "it won't hurt to take out a little of this and pour it on the ground. It ought to be good fertilizer." He stooped. "'Come, gentle spring, ethereal mildness, come,'" he quoted, and dipped in the pail.

Just then somebody fell against the door and stumbled into the room. It was Tillie, as white as milk, and breathing in gasps.

"Quick!" she screeched, "Minnie, quick!"

"What is it?" I asked, jumping up. She'd fallen back against the door-frame and stood with her hand clutching her heart.

"That dev—devil—Mike!" she panted. "He has turned on the steam in the men's baths and gone—gone away!"

"With people in the bath?" Doctor Barnes asked, slamming down the pail.

Tillie nodded.

"Then why in creation don't they get out of the baths until we can shut off the steam?" I demanded, grabbing up my shawl. But Tillie shook her head in despair.

"They can't," she answered, "he's hid their clothes!"

The next thing I recall is running like mad up the walk with Doctor Barnes beside me, steadying me by the arm. I only spoke once that I remember and that was just as we got to the house,

"This settles it!" I panted, desperately. "It's all over."

"Not a bit of it!" he said, shoving me up the steps and into the hall. "The old teakettle is just getting 'het up' a bit. By the gods and little fishes, just listen to it singing down there!"

The help was gathered in a crowd at the head of the bath-house staircase, where a cloud of steam was coming up, and down below we could hear furious talking, and somebody shouting, "Mike! Mike!" in a voice that was choked with rage and steam.

Doctor Barnes elbowed his way through the crowd to the top of the stairs and I followed.

"There's Minnie!" Amanda King yelled. "She knows all about the place. Minnie, you can shut it off, can't you?"

"I'll try," I said, and was starting down, when Doctor Barnes jerked me back.

"You stay here," he said. "Where's Mr. Pier—where's Carter?"

"Down with the engineer," somebody replied out of the steam cloud.

"Hello there!" he called down the staircase. "How's the air?"

"Clothes! Send us some clothes!"

It was Mr. Sam calling. The rest was swallowed up in a fresh roaring, as if a steam-pipe had given away. That settled the people below. With a burst of fury they swarmed up the stairs in their bath sheets, the bishop leading, and just behind him, talking as no gentleman should talk under any circumstances, Senator Biggs. The rest followed, their red faces shining through the steam—all of them murderous, holding their sheets around them with one hand, and waving the other in a frenzy. It was awful.

The help scattered and ran, but I stood my ground. The sight of a man in a sheet didn't scare me and it was no time for weakness.

The steam was thicker than ever, and the hall was misty. A moment later the engineer came up and after him Mr. Pierce, with a towel over his mouth and a screw-driver in his hand. He was white with rage. He brushed past the sheets without paying the slightest attention to them, and tore the towel off his mouth.

"Who saw Mike last?" he shouted across to where the pharmacy clerk, the elevator boy and some of the bell-boys had retreated to the office and were peeping out through the door.

Here Mr. Moody, who's small at any time, and who without the padding on his shoulders and wrapped in a sheet with his red face above, looked like a lighted cigarette, darted out of the crowd and caught him by the sleeve.

"Here!" he cried, "we've got a few things to say to you, you young—"

"Take your hand off my arm!" thundered Mr. Pierce.

The storm broke with that. They crowded around Mr. Pierce, yelling like maniacs, and he stood there, white-faced, and let them wear themselves out. The courage of a man in a den of lions was nothing to it. Doctor Barnes forced his way through the crowd and stood there beside him.

It wasn't only the steam and their clothes being hidden; it had started with the scare at the spring in the morning, and when they had told him what they thought about that, they went back still further and bellowed about the mismanagement of the place ever since he had taken charge, and the food, and the steam-heat, and the new rules—oh, they hated him all right, and they told him so, purple-faced with rage and heat, dancing around him and shaking one fist in his face, as I say, while they held their sheets fast with the other.

And I stood there and watched, my mind awhirl, expecting every minute to hear that they were all leaving, or to have some one forget and shake both fists at once.

And that's how it ended finally—I mean, of course, that they said they would all leave immediately, and that he ought to be glad to have them go quietly, and not have him jailed for malicious mischief or compounding a felony. The whole thing was an outrage, and the three train would leave the house as empty as a squeezed lemon.

I wanted to go forward and drop on my knees and implore them to remember the old doctor, and the baths they'd had when nothing went wrong, and the days when they'd sworn that the spring kept them young and well, but there was something in Mr. Pierce's face that kept me back.

"At three o'clock, then," he said. "Very well."

"Don't be a fool!" I heard Mr. Sam from the crowd.

"Is that all you have to say?" roared Mr. von Inwald. I hadn't noticed him before. He had his sheet on in Grecian style and it looked quite ornamental although a little short. "Haven't you any apology to make, sir?"

"Neither apology nor explanation to you," Mr. Pierce retorted. And to the other: "It is an unfortunate accident—incident, if you prefer." He looked at Thoburn, who was the only one in a bath robe, and who was the only cheerful one in the lot. "I had refused a request of the bath man's and he has taken this form of revenge. If this gives me the responsibility I am willing to take it. If you expect me to ask you to stay I'll not do it. I don't mind saying that I am as tired of all this as you are."

"As tired of what?" demanded Mr. Moody, pushing forward out of the crowd. Mr. Sam was making frantic gestures to catch Mr. Pierce's eye, but he would not look at him.

"Of all this," he said. "Of charging people sanatorium prices under a pretense of making them well. Does anybody here imagine he's going to find health by sitting around in an overstuffed leather chair, with the temperature at eighty, eating five meals a day, and walking as far as the mineral spring for exercise?"

There was a sort of angry snarl in the air, and Mr. Sam threw up his one free hand in despair.

"In fact," Mr. Pierce went on, "I'd about decided on a new order of things for this place anyhow. It's going to be a real health resort, run for people who want to get well or keep well. People who wish to be overfed, overheated and coddled need not come—or stay."

The bishop spoke over the heads of the others, who looked dazed.

"Does that mean," he inquired mildly, "that—guests must either obey this new order of things or go away?"

Mr. Pierce looked at the bishop and smiled.

"I'm sorry, sir," he said, "but as every one is leaving, anyhow—"

They fairly jumped at him then. They surrounded him in a howling mob and demanded how he dared to turn them out, and what did he mean by saying they were overfed, and they would leave when they were good and ready and not before, and he could go to blazes. It was the most scandalous thing I've ever known of at Hope Springs, and in the midst of it Mr. Pierce stood cool and quiet, waiting for a chance to speak. And when the time came he jumped in and told them the truth about themselves, and most of it hurt.

He was good and mad, and he stood there and picked out the flabby ones and the fat ones, the whisky livers and the tobacco hearts and the banquet stomachs, and called them out by name.

When he got through they were standing in front of him, ashamed to look at one another, and not knowing whether to fall on him and tear him to pieces, or go and weep in a corner because they'd played such havoc with the bodies the Lord gave them. If he'd weakened for a minute they'd have jumped on him. But he didn't. He got through and stood looking at them in their sheets, and then he said coolly:

"The bus will be ready at two-thirty, gentlemen," and turning on his heels, went into the office and closed the door.

They scattered to their rooms in every stage of rage and excitement, and at last only Mr. Sam and I were left staring at each other. "Damned young idiot!" he said. "I wish to heavens you'd never suggested bringing him here, Minnie!"

And leaving me speechless with indignation, he trailed himself and his sheet up the stairs.

CHAPTER XXII

HOME TO ROOST

I couldn't stand any more. It was all over! I rushed to my room and threw myself on the bed. At two-thirty I heard the bus come to the porte-cochere under my window and then drive away; that was the last straw. I put a pillow over my head so nobody could hear me, and then and there I had hysterics. I knew I was having them, and I wasn't ashamed. I'd have exploded if I hadn't. And then somebody jerked the pillow away and I looked up, with my eyes swollen almost shut, and it was Doctor Barnes. He had a glass of water in his hand and he held it right above me.

"One more yell," he said, "and it goes over you!"

I lay there staring up at him, and then I knew what a fright I looked, and although I couldn't speak yet, I reached up and felt for my hairpins.

"That's better," he said, putting down the glass. "Another ten minutes of that and you'd have burst a blood vessel. Don't worry. I know I have no business here, but I anticipated something of this kind, and it may interest you to know that I've been outside in the hall since the first whoop. It's been a good safety-valve."

I sat up and stared at him. I could hardly see out of my eyes. He had his back to the light, but I could tell that he had a cross of adhesive plaster on his cheek and that one eye was almost shut. He smiled when he saw my expression.

"It's the temperament," he said. "It goes with the hair. I've got it too, only I'm apt to go out and pick a fight at such times, and a woman hasn't got that outlet. As you see, I found Mike, and my disfigurement is to Mike's as starlight to the noonday glare. Come and take a walk."

I shook my head, but he took my arm and pulled me off the bed.

"You come for a walk!" he said. "I'll wait in the hall until you powder your nose. You look like a fire that's been put out by a rain-storm."

I didn't want to go, but anything was better than sitting in the room moping. I put on my jacket and Miss Patty's chinchillas, which cheered me a little, but as we went downstairs the quiet of the place sat on my chest like a weight.

The lower hall was empty. A new card headed "Rules" hung on the door into the private office, but I did not read it. What was the use of rules without people to disobey them? Mrs. Moody had forgotten her crocheting bag and it hung on the back of a chair. I had to bite my lip to keep it from trembling again.

"The Jenningses are still here," said the doctor. "The old man is madder than any hornet ever dared be, and they go in the morning. But the situation was too much for our German friend. He left with the others."

Well, we went out and I took the path I knew best, which was out toward the spring-house. There wasn't a soul in sight. The place looked lonely, with the trees hung with snow, and arching over the board walk. At the little bridge over the creek Doctor Barnes stopped, and leaning over the rail, took a good look at me.

"When you self-contained women go to pieces," he said, "you pretty near smash, don't you? You look as if you'd had a death in your family."

"This WAS my family," I half sniveled.

"But," he said, "you'll be getting married and having a home of your own and forgetting all about this."

He looked at me with his sharp eyes. "There's probably some nice chap in the village, eh?"

I shook my head. I had just caught sight of the broken pieces of the Moody water-pitcher on the ice below.

"No nice young man!" he remarked. "Not the telegraph operator, or the fellow who runs the livery-stable—I've forgotten his name."

"Look here," I turned on him, "if you're talking all this nonsense to keep my mind off things, you needn't."

"I'm not," he said. "I'm asking for the sake of my own mind, but we'll not bother about that now. We'd better start back."

It was still snowing, although not so hard. The air had done me some good, but the lump in my throat seemed to have gone to my chest. The doctor helped me along, for the snow was drifting, and when he saw I was past the crying stage he went back to what we were both thinking about.

"Old Pierce is right," he said. "Remember, Miss Minnie, I've nothing against you or your mineral spring; in fact, I'm strong for you both. But while I'm out of the ring now for good—I don't mind saying to you what I said to Pierce, that the only thing that gets into training here, as far as I can see, is a fellow's pocketbook."

We went back to the house and I straightened the news stand, Amanda King having taken a violent toothache as a result of the excitement. The Jenningses were packing to go, and Miss Summers had got a bottle of peroxide and shut herself in her room. At six o'clock Tillie beckoned to me from the door of the officers' dining-room and said she'd put the basket in the snow by the grape arbor. I got ready, with a heavy heart, to take it out. I had forgotten all about their dinner, for one thing, and I had to carry bad news.

But Mr. Pierce had been there before me. I saw tracks in the fresh snow, for, praise heaven! it had snowed all that week and our prints were filled up almost as fast as we made them. When I got to the shelter-house it was in a wild state of excitement. Mrs. Dick, with her cheeks flushed, had gathered all her things on the cot and was rolling them up in sheets and newspapers. But Mr. Dick was sitting on the box in front of the fire with his curly hair standing every way. He had been roasting potatoes, and as I opened the door, he picked one up and poked at it to see if it was done.

"Damn!" he said, and dropped it.

Mrs. Dick sat on the cot rolling up a pink ribbon and looked at him.

"If you want to know exactly my reason for insisting on moving to-night, I'll tell you," she said, paying no attention to me. "It is your disposition."

He didn't say anything, but he put his foot on the potato and smashed it.

"If I had to be shut in here with you one more day," she went on, "I'd hate you."

"Why the one more day?" he asked, without looking up.

But she didn't answer him. She was in the worst kind of a temper; she threw the ribbon down, and coming over, lifted the lid of my basket and looked in.

"Ham again!" she exclaimed ungratefully. "Thanks so much for remembering us, Minnie. I dare say our dinner to-day slipped your mind!"

"I wonder if it strikes you, Minnie," Mr. Dick said, noticing me for the first time, "that if you and Sam hadn't been so confounded meddling, that fellow Pierce would be washing buggies in the village livery-stable where he belongs, and I'd be in one piece of property that's as good as gone this minute."

"Egg salad and cheese!" said Mrs. Dick. "I'm sick of cheese. If that's the kind of supper you've been serving—"

But I was in a bad humor, anyhow, and I'd had enough. I stood just inside the door and I told them I'd done the best I could, not for them, but because I'd promised the old doctor, and if I'd made mistakes I'd answer for them to him if I ever met him in the next world. And in the meantime I washed my hands of the whole thing, and they might make out as best they could. I was going.

Mrs. Dick heard me through. Then she came over and put her hand on mine where it lay on the table.

"You're perfectly right," she said. "I know how you have tried, and that the fault is all that wretched Pierce's. You mustn't mind Mr. Carter, Minnie. He's been in that sort of humor all day."

He looked at her with the most miserable face I ever saw, but he didn't say anything. She sighed, the little wretch.

"We've all made mistakes," she said, "and not the least was my thinking that I—well, never mind. I dare say we will manage somehow."

He got up then, his face twisted with misery.

"Say it," he said. "You hate me; you shiver if I touch your hand—oh, I'm not very keen, but I saw that."

"The remedy for that is very, simple," she replied coolly. "You needn't touch my hand."

"Stop!" I snapped. "Just stop before you say something you'll be sorry for. Of course, you hate each other. It beats me, anyhow, why two people who get married always want to get away by themselves until they're so sick of each other that they don't get over it the rest of their lives. The only sensible honeymoon I ever heard of was when one of the chambermaids here married a farmer in the neighborhood. It was harvest and he couldn't leave, so she went ALONE to see her folks and she said it beat having him along all hollow."

She was setting out the supper, putting things down with a bang. He didn't move, although he must have been starving.

"Another thing I'd advise," I said. "Eat first and talk after. You'll see things different after you've got something in your stomach."

"I wish you wouldn't meddle, Minnie!" she snapped, and having put down her own plate and knife and fork, not laying a place for him, she went over and tried to get one of the potatoes from the fire.

Well, she burnt her finger, or pretended to, and I guess her solution was as good as mine, for she began to cry, and when I left he was tying it up with a bit of his handkerchief; if she shivered when he kissed it I didn't notice it. They were to come up to the house after her father left in the morning, and I was to dismiss all the old help and get new ones so he could take charge and let Mr. Pierce go.

I plodded back with my empty basket. I had only one clear thought,—that I wouldn't have any more tramping across the golf links in the snow. I was too tired really to care that with the regular winter boarders gone and eight weeks still until Lent, we'd hardly be able to keep going another fortnight. I wanted to get back to my room and go to bed and forget.

But as I came near the house I saw Mr. Pierce come out on the front piazza and switch on the lights. He stood there looking out into the snow, and the next minute I saw why. Coming up the hill and across the lawn was a shadowy line of people, black against the white. They were not speaking, and they moved without noise over the snow. I thought for a minute that my brain had gone wrong; then the first figure came into the light, and it was the bishop. He stood at the front of the steps and looked up at Mr. Pierce.

"I dare say," he said, trying to look easy, "that this is sooner than you expected us!"

Mr. Pierce looked down at the crowd. Then he smiled, a growing smile that ended in a grin.

"On the contrary," he said, "I've been expecting you for an hour or more."

The procession began to move gloomily up the steps. All of them carried hand luggage, and they looked tired and sheepish Miss Cobb stopped in front of Mr. Pierce.

"Do you mean to say," she demanded furiously, "that you knew the railroad was blocked with snow, and yet you let us go!"

"On the contrary, Miss Cobb," he said politely, "I remember distinctly regretting that you insisted on going. Besides, there was the Sherman House."

Senator Briggs {sic} stopped in front of him. "Probably you also knew that THAT was full, including the stables, with people from the stalled trains," he asserted furiously.

Two by two they went in and through the hall, stamping the snow off, and up to their old rooms again, leaving Slocum, the clerk, staring at them as if he couldn't believe his eyes.

Mr. Pierce and I watched from the piazza, through the glass.

We saw Doctor Barnes stop and look, and then go and hang over the news stand and laugh himself almost purple, and we saw Mr. Thoburn bringing up the tail of the procession and trying to look unconcerned. I am not a revengeful woman, but that was one of the happiest moments of my life.

Doctor Barnes turned suddenly, and catching me by the arm, whirled me around and around, singing wildly something about Noah and "the animals went in two by, two, the elephant and the kangaroo."

He stopped as suddenly as he began and walked me to the door again.

"We've got 'em in the ark," he said, "but I'm thinking this forty days of snow is nearly over, Minnie. I don't think much of the dove and the olive-branch, but WE'VE GOT TO KEEP THEM."

"It's against the law," I quavered.

"Nonsense!" he said. "We've got to make 'em WANT to stay!"

CHAPTER XXIII

BACK TO NATURE

We gave them a good supper and Mr. Pierce ordered claret served without extra charge. By eight o'clock they were all in better humor, and when they'd gathered in the lobby Miss Summers gave an imitation of Marie Dressler doing the Salome dance. Every now and then somebody would look out and say it was still snowing, and with the memory of the drifts and the cold stove in the railroad station behind them, they'd gather closer around the fire and insist that they would go as soon as the road was cleared.

But with the exception of Mr. von Inwald, not one of them really wanted to go. As Doctor Barnes said over the news stand, each side was bluffing and wouldn't call the other, and the fellow with the most nerve would win.

"And, oh, my aunt!" he said, "what a sweet disposition the von Inwald has! Watch him going up and banging his head against the wall!"

Everybody was charmed with the Salome dance, especially when Miss Summers drew the cover off a meat platter she'd been dancing around, and there was Arabella sitting on her hind legs, with a card tied to her neck, and the card said that at eleven there would be a clambake in the kitchen for all the guests.

The clambake was my idea, but the dog, of course, was Miss Julia's. I never saw a woman so full of ideas, although it seems that what should have been on the platter was the head of somebody or other.

Just after the dance I saw Mr. von Inwald talking to Miss Patty. He had been ugly all evening, and now he looked like a devil. She stood facing him with her head thrown back and her fingers twisting her ruby ring. I guessed that she was about as much surprised as anything else, people having a habit of being pleasant to her most of the time. He left her in a rage, and as he went he collided with Arabella and kicked her. Miss Patty went white but Miss Summers was not a bit put out. She simply picked up the howling dog and confronted Mr. von Inwald.

"Perhaps you didn't notice," she said sweetly, "but you kicked my dog."

"Why don't you keep her out of the way?" he snarled, and they stood glaring at each other.

"Under the circumstances, Arabella," Miss Julia said—and everybody was listening—"we can only withdraw Mr. von Inwald's invitation to the kitchen."

"Thank you, I had not intended to go," he said furiously, and went out into the veranda, slamming the door behind him. Mr. Jennings looked up from where he was playing chess by the fire and nodded at Miss Summers.

"Serves him right for his temper!" he said.

"Checkmate!" said the bishop.

Mr. Jennings turned and glared at the board. Then with one sweep he threw all the chessmen on the floor. As Tillie said later, it would be a pity to spoil two houses with Mr. von Inwald and Mr. Jennings If they were in the same family, they could work it off on each other.

Miss Patty came down to the news stand and pretended to hunt for a magazine. I reached over and stroked her hand. "Don't take it too hard, dearie," I said. "He's put out to-night, and maybe he isn't well. Men are like babies. If their stomachs are all right and have plenty in them, they're pleasant enough. It's been my experience that your cranky man's a sick man."

"I don't think he is sick, Minnie," she said, with a catch in her voice. "I—I think he is just dev—devilish!"

Well, I thought that too, so I just stroked her hand, and after a minute she got her color again. "It is hard for him," she said. "He thinks this is all vulgar and American, and—oh, Minnie, I want to get away, and yet what shall I do without you to keep me sensible."

"You'll be a long ways off soon," I said, touching the ring under my hand.

"I wish you could come with me," she said, but I shook my head.

"Here is one dog that isn't going to sit under any rich man's table and howl for crumbs," I answered. "If he kicked ME, I'd bite him."

At eleven o'clock we had the clambake with beer in the kitchen, and Mr. von Inwald came, after all. They were really very cheerful, all of them. Doctor Barnes insisted that Senator Biggs must not fast any longer, and he ate by my count three dozen clams. At the end, when everybody was happy and everything forgiven, Mr. Pierce got up and made a speech.

He said he was sorry for what had happened that day, but that much he had said he still maintained: that to pretend to make people well in the way most sanatoriums did it was sheer folly, and he felt his responsibility too keenly to countenance a system that was clearly wrong and that the best modern thought considered obsolete.

Miss Cobb sat up at that; she is always talking about the best modern thought.

He said that perfect health, clear skins, bright eyes—he looked at the women, and except for Miss Patty, there wasn't an honest complexion or a bright eye in the lot—keen appetites and joy of living all depended on rational and simple living.

"Hear, hear!" said the men.

"The nearer we live to nature, the better," said Senator Biggs oracularly.

"Back to nature," shouted Mr. Moody through a clam.

"Exactly," Mr. Pierce said, smiling.

Mrs. Moody looked alarmed. "You don't mean doing without clothes—and all that!" she protested.

"Surely!" Miss Summers said, holding up her beer glass. "A toast, everybody! Back to nature, sans rats, sans rouge, sans stays, sans everything. I'll need to wear a tag with my name on it. Nobody will recognize me!"

Mr. Pierce got up again at the head of the long kitchen table and said he merely meant rational living—more air, more exercise, simpler food and better hours. It was being done now in a thousand fresh-air farms, and succeeding. Men went back to their business clearer-headed and women grew more beautiful.

At that, what with the reaction from sitting in the cold station, and the beer and everything, they all grew enthusiastic. Doctor Barnes made a speech, telling that he used to be puny and weak, and how he went into training and became a pugilist, and how he'd fought the Tennessee something or other—the men nodded as if they knew—and licked him in forty seconds or forty rounds, I'm not sure which. The men were standing on their chairs cheering for him, and even Mr. Jennings, who'd been sitting and not saying much, said he thought probably there was something in it.

They ended by agreeing to try it out for a week, beginning with the morning, when everybody was to be down for breakfast by seven-thirty. Mr. Thoburn got up and made a speech, protesting that they didn't know what they were letting themselves in for, and ended up by demanding to know if he was expected to breakfast at seven-thirty.

"Yes, or earlier," Mr. Pierce said pleasantly. "I suppose you could have something at seven."

"And suppose I refuse?" he retorted disagreeably.

But everybody turned on him, and said if they could do it, he could, and he sat down again. Then somebody suggested that if they were to get up they'd have to go to bed, and the party broke up.

Doctor Barnes helped me gather up the clam shells and the plates.

"It's a risky business," he said. "To-night doesn't mean anything; they're carried away by the reaction and the desire for something new. The next week will tell the tale."

"If we could only get rid of Mr. Thoburn!" I exclaimed. Doctor Barnes chuckled.

"We may not get rid of him," he said, "but I can promise him the most interesting week of his life. He'll be too busy for mischief. I'm going to take six inches off his waist line."

Well, in a half-hour or so I had cleared away, and I went out to the lobby to lock up the news stand. Just as I opened the door from the back hall, however, I heard two people talking.

It was Miss Pat and Mr. Pierce. She was on the stairs and he in the hall below, looking up.

"I don't WANT to stay!" she was saying.

"But don't you see?" he argued. "If you go, the others will. Can't you try it for a week?"

"I quite understand your motive," she said, looking down at him more pleasantly than she'd ever done, "and it's very good of you and all that. But if you'd only left things as they were, and let us all go, and other people come—"

"That's just it," he said. "I'm told it's the bad season and nobody else would come until Lent. And, anyhow, it's not business to let a lot of people go away mad. It gives the place a black eye."

"Dear me," she said, "how businesslike you are growing!"

He went over close to the stairs and dropped his voice.

"If you want the bitter truth," he went on, trying to smile, "I've put myself on trial and been convicted of being a fool and a failure. I've failed regularly and with precision at everything I have tried. I've been going around so long trying to find a place that I fit into, that I'm scarred as with many battles. And now I'm on probation—for the last time. If this doesn't go, I—I—"

"What?" she asked, leaning down to him. "You'll not—"

"Oh, no," he said, "nothing dramatic, of course. I could go around the country in a buggy selling lightning-rods—"

She drew herself back as if she resented his refusal of her sympathy.

"Or open a saloon in the Philippines!" he finished mockingly. "There's a living in that."

"You are impossible," she said, and turned away.

Oh, I haven't any excuse to make for him! I think he was just hungry for her sympathy and her respect, knowing nothing else was coming to him. But the minute they grew a bit friendly he seemed to remember the prince, and that, according to his idea of it, she was selling herself, and he would draw off and look at her in a mocking unhappy way that made me want to slap him.

He watched her up the stairs and then turned and walked to the fire, with his hands in his pockets and his head down.

I closed the news stand and he came over just as I was hanging up the cigar-case key for Amanda King in the morning. He reached up and took the key off its nail.

"I'll keep that," he said. "It's no tobacco after this, Minnie."

"You can't keep them here, then," I retorted. "They've got to smoke; it's the only work they do."

"We'll see," he said quietly. "And—oh, yes, Minnie, now that we shall not be using the mineral spring—"

"Not use the mineral spring!" I repeated, stupefied.

"Certainly NOT!" he said. "This is a drugless sanatorium, Minnie, from now on. That's part of the theory—no drugs."

"Well, I'll tell you one thing," I snapped, "theory or no theory, you've got to have drugs. No theory that I ever heard of is going to cure Mr. Moody's indigestion and Miss Cobb's neuralgia."

"They won't have indigestion and neuralgia."

"Or Amanda King's toothache."

"We won't have Amanda King."

He put his elbow on the stand and smiled at me.

"Listen, Minnie," he said. "If you hadn't been wasting your abilities in the mineral spring, I'd be sorry to close it. But there will be plenty for you to do. Don't you know that the day of the medicine-closet in the bath-room and the department-store patent-remedy counter is over? We've got sanatoriums now instead of family doctors. In other words, we put in good sanitation systems and don't need the plumber and his repair kit."

"The pharmacy?" I said between my teeth.

"Closed also. No medicine, Minnie. That's our slogan. This is the day of prophylaxis. The doctors have taken a step in the right direction and are giving fewer drugs. Christian Science has abolished drugs and established the healer. We simply abolish the healer."

"If we're not going to use the spring-house, we might have saved the expense of the new roof in the fall," I said bitterly.

"Not at all. For two hours or so a day the spring-house will be a rest-house—windows wide open and God's good air penetrating to fastnesses it never knew before."

"The spring will freeze!"

"Exactly. My only regret is that it is too small to skate on. But they'll have the ice pond."

"When I see Mr. Moody skating on the ice pond," I said sarcastically, "I'll see Mrs. Moody dead with the shock on the bank."

"Not at all," he replied calmly. "You'll see her skating, too." And with that he went to bed.

CHAPTER XXIV

LIKE DUCKS TO WATER

They took to it like ducks take to water. Not, of course, that they didn't kick about making their own beds and having military discipline generally. They complained a lot, but when after three days went by with the railroad running as much on schedule as it ever does, they were all still there, and Mr. Jennings had limped out and spent a half-hour at the wood-pile with his gouty foot on a cushion, I saw it was a success.

I ought to have been glad. I was, although when Mrs. Dicky found they were all staying, and that she might have to live in the shelter-house the rest of the winter, there was an awful scene. I was glad, too, every time I could see Mr. Thoburn's gloomy face, or hear the things he said when his name went up for the military walk.

Oh yes, we had a blackboard in the hall, and every morning each guest looked to see if it was wood-pile day or military-walk day. At first, instead of wood-pile, it was walk-clearing day, but they soon had the snow off all the paths.

As I say, I was glad. It looked as if the new idea was a success, although as Doctor Barnes said, nobody could really tell until new people began to come. That was the real test. They had turned the baths into a gymnasium and they had beginners' classes and advanced classes, and a prize offered on the blackboard of a cigar for the man who made the most muscular improvement in a week. The bishop won it the first week, being the only one who could lie on his back and raise himself to a sitting position without helping himself with his hands. As Mrs. Moody said, it would be easy enough if somebody only sat on one's feet to hold them down.

But I must say I never got over the shock of seeing the spring-house drifted with snow, all the windows wide open, the spring frozen hard, and people sitting there during the rest hour, in furs and steamer rugs, trying to play cards with mittens on—their hands, not the cards, of course—and not wrangling. I was lonesome for it!

I hadn't much to do, except from two to four to be at the spring-house, and to count for the deep-breathing exercise. Oh, yes, we had that, too! I rang a bell every half-hour and everybody got up, and I counted slowly "one" and they breathed in through their noses, and "two" and they exhaled quickly through their mouths. I guess most of them used more of their lungs than they ever knew they had.

Well, everybody looked better and felt better, although they wouldn't all acknowledge it. Miss Cobb suffered most, not having the fire log to curl her hair with. But as she said herself, between gymnasium and military walks, and the silence hour, and eating, which took a long time, everybody being hungry—and going to bed at nine, she didn't see how she could have worried with it, anyhow. The fat ones, of course, objected to an apple and a cup of hot water for breakfast, but except Mr. Thoburn, they all realized it was for the best. He wasn't there for his health, he said, having never had a sick day in his life, but when he saw it was apple and hot water or leave, he did like Adam—he took the apple.

The strange thing of all was the way they began to look up to Mr. Pierce. He was very strict; if he made a rule, it was obey or leave. As they knew after Mr. Moody refused to take the military walk, and was presented with his bill and a railroad schedule within an hour. He had to take the military walk with

Doctor Barnes that afternoon alone. They had to respect a man who could do all the things in the gymnasium that they couldn't, and come in from a ten or fifteen-mile tramp through the snow and take a cold plunge and a swim to rest himself.

It was on Monday that we really got things started, and on Monday afternoon Miss Summers came out to the shelter-house in a towering rage.

"Where's Mr. Pierce?" she demanded.

"I guess you can see he isn't here," I said.

"Just wait until I see him!" she announced. "Do you know that I am down on the blackboard for the military walk to-day?

"Why not?"

She turned and glared at me. "Why not?" she repeated. "Why, the audacity of the wretch! He brings me out into the country in winter to play in his atrocious play, strands me, and then tells me to walk twenty miles a day and smile over it!" She came over to me and shook my arm. "Not only that," she said, "but he has cut out my cigarettes and put Arabella on dog biscuit—Arabella, who can hardly eat a chicken wing."

"Well, there's something to be thankful for," I said. "He didn't put you on dog biscuit."

She laughed then, with one of her quick changes of humor.

"The worst of it is," she said, in a confidential whisper, "I'll do it. I feel it. I guess if the truth were known I'm some older than he is, but—I'm afraid of him, Minnie. Little Judy is ready to crawl around and speak for a cracker or a kind word. Oh, I'm not in love with him, but he's got the courage to say what he means and do what he says."

She went to the door and looked back smiling.

"I'm off for the wood-pile," she called back. "And I've promised to chop two inches off my heels."

As I say, they took to it like ducks to water—except two of them, von Inwald and Thoburn. Mr. von Inwald stayed on, I hardly know why, but I guess it was because Mr. Jennings still hadn't done anything final about settlements, and with the newspapers marrying him every day it wasn't very comfortable. Next to him, Mr. Thoburn was the unhappiest mortal I have ever seen. He wouldn't leave, and with Doctor Barnes carrying out his threat to take six inches off his waist, he stopped measuring window-frames with a tape line and took to measuring himself.

I came across him on Wednesday—the third day—straggling home from the military walk. He and Mr. von Inwald limped across the tennis-court and collapsed on the steps of the spring-house while the others went on to the sanatorium. I had been brushing the porch, and I leaned on my broom and looked at them.

"You're both looking a lot better," I said. "Not so—well, not so beer-y. How do you like it by this time?"

"Fine!" answered Mr. Thoburn. "Wouldn't stay if I didn't like it."

"Wouldn't you?"

"But I'll tell you this, Minnie," he said, changing his position with a groan to look up at me, "somebody ought to warn that young man. Human nature can stand a lot but it can't stand everything. He's overdoing it!"

"They like it," I said.

"They think they do," he retorted. "Mark my words, Minnie, if he adds another mile to the walk to-morrow there will be a mutiny. Kingdoms may be lost by an extra blister on a heel."

Mr. von Inwald had been sitting with his feet straight out, scowling, but now he turned and looked at me coolly.

"All that keeps me here," he said, "is Minnie's lovely hair. It takes me mentally back home, Minnie, to a lovely lady—may I have a bit of it to keep by me?"

"You may not," I retorted angrily.

"Oh! The lovely lady—but never mind that. For the sake of my love for you, Minnie, find me a cigarette, like a good girl! I am desolate."

"There's no tobacco on the place," I said firmly, and went on with my sweeping.

"When I was a boy," Mr. Thoburn remarked, looking out thoughtfully over the snow, "we made a sort of cigarette out of corn-silk. You don't happen to have any corn-silk about, do you, Minnie?"

"No," I said shortly. "If you take my advice, Mr. Thoburn, you'll go back to town. You can get all the tobacco you want there—and you're wasting your time here." I leaned on my broom and looked down at him, but he was stretching out his foot and painfully working his ankle up and down.

"Am I?" he asked, looking at his foot. "Well, don't count on it too much, Minnie. You always inspire me, and sitting here I've just thought of something."

He got up and hobbled off the porch, followed by Mr. von Inwald. I saw him say something to Mr. von Inwald, who threw back his head and laughed. Then I saw them stop and shake hands and go on again in deep conversation. I felt uneasy.

Doctor Barnes came out that afternoon and watched me while I closed the windows. He had a package in his hand. He sat on the railing of the spring and looked at me.

"You're not warmly enough dressed for this kind of thing," he remarked. "Where's that gray rabbits' fur, or whatever it is?"

"If you mean my chinchillas," I said, "they're in their box. Chinchillas are as delicate as babies and not near so plentiful. I'm warm enough."

"You look it." He reached over and caught one of my hands. "Look at that! Blue nails! It's about four degrees above zero here, and while the rest are wrapped in furs and steamer rugs, with hotwater bottles at their feet, you've got on a shawl. I'll bet you two dollars you haven't got on any—er—winter flannels."

"I never bet," I retorted, and went on folding up the steamer rugs.

"I'd like to help," he said, "but you're so darned capable, Miss Minnie—"

"You might see if you can get the slot-machine empty," I said. "It's full of water. It wouldn't work and Mr. Moody thought it was frozen. He's been carrying out boiling water all afternoon. If it stays in there and freezes the thing will explode."

He wasn't listening. He'd been fussing with his package and now he opened it and handed it to me, in the paper.

"It's a sweater," he said, not looking at me. "I bought it for myself and it was too small— Confound it, Minnie, I wish I could lie! I bought them for you! There's the whole business—sweater, cap, leggings and mittens. Go on! Throw them at me!"

But I didn't. I looked at them, all white and soft, and it came over me suddenly how kind people had been lately, and how much I'd been getting—the old doctor's waistcoat buttons and Miss Pat's furs, and now this! I just buried my face in them and cried.

Doctor Barnes stood by and said nothing. Some men wouldn't have understood, but he did. After a minute or so he came over and pulled the sweater out from the bundle.

"I'm glad you like 'em," he said, "but as I bought them at Hubbard's, in Finleyville, and as the old liar guaranteed they wouldn't shrink, we'd better not cry on 'em."

Well, I put them on and I was warmer and happier than I had been for some time. But that night when I went out to the shelter-house with the supper basket I found both the honeymooners in a wild state of excitement. They said that about five o'clock Thoburn had gone out to the shelter-house and walked all around it. Finally he had stopped at one of the windows of the other room, had worked at it with his penknife and got it open, and crawled through. They sat paralyzed with fright, and heard him moving around the other room, and he even tried their door. But it had been locked. They hadn't the slightest idea what he was doing, but after perhaps ten minutes he went away, going out the door this time and taking the key with him.

Mr. Dick had gone in when he was safely gone, but he could see nothing unusual, except that the door of the cupboard in the corner was standing open and there was a brand-new, folding, foot rule in it.

That day the bar was closed for good, and there was a good bit of fussing. To add to the trouble, that evening at dinner the pastries were cut off, and at eight o'clock a delegation headed by Senator Biggs visited Mr. Pierce in the office and demanded pastry put back on the menu and the stewed fruit taken off. But Mr. Pierce was firm and they came out pretty well subdued. It was that night, I think, that candles were put in the bedrooms, and all the electric lights were turned off at nine-thirty.

At ten o'clock I took my candle and went to Mr. Pierce's sitting-room door. I didn't think they'd stand much more and I wanted to tell him so. Nobody answered and I opened the door. He was asleep, face down on the hearth-rug in front of the fire. His candle was lighted on the floor beside him and near it lay a newspaper cutting crumpled in a ball. I picked it up. It was a list of the bridal party for Miss Patty's wedding.

I dropped it where I found it and went out and knocked again loudly. He wakened after a minute and came to the door with the candle in his hand.

"Oh, it's you, Minnie. Come in!"

I went in and put my candle on the table.

"I've got to talk to you," I said. "I don't mind admitting things have been going pretty well, but—they won't stand for the candles. You mark my words."

"If they'll stand for the bar being closed, why not the candles?" he demanded.

"Well," I said, "they can't have electric light sent up in boxes and labeled 'books,' but they can get liquor that way."

He whistled, and then he laughed.

"Then we'll not have any books," he said. "I guess they can manage. 'My only books were woman's looks—'" and then he saw the ball of paper on the floor and his expression changed. He walked over and picked it up, smoothing it out on the palm of his hand.

After a minute he looked up at me.

"I haven't been to the shelter-house to-day. They are all right?"

"They're nervous. With everybody walking these days they daren't venture a nose out of doors."

He was still holding the clipping.

"And—Miss Jennings!" he said. "She—I think she looks better."

"Her father's in a better humor for one thing—says Abraham Lincoln split logs, and that it beats massage."

I had been standing in the doorway, but he took me by the arm and drew me into the room.

"I wish you'd sit down for about ten minutes, Minnie," he said. "I guess every fellow has a time when he's got to tell his troubles to some good woman—not but that you know mine already. You're as shrewd as you are kind."

I sat down on the edge of a chair. For all I had had so much to do with the sanatorium, I never forgot that I was only the spring-house girl. He threw himself back in his easy chair, with the candle behind him on the table and his arms above his head.

"It's like this, Minnie," he said. "Mr. Jennings likes the new order of things and—he's going to stay."

I nodded.

"And I like it here. I want to stay. It's the one thing I've found that I think I can do. It isn't what I've dreamed of, but it's worth while. To anchor the derelicts of humanity in a sort of repair dock here, and scrape the barnacles off their dispositions, and send them out shipshape again, surely that's something. And I can do it."

I nodded again.

"But if the Jenningses stay—" he looked at me. "Minnie, in heaven's name, what am I going to do if SHE stays?"

"I don't know, Mr. Pierce," I said. "I couldn't sleep last night for thinking about it."

He smoothed out the paper and looked at it again, but I think he scarcely saw it.

"The situation is humorous," he said, "only my sense of humor seems to have died. She doesn't know I exist, except to invent new and troublesome regulations for her annoyance. She is very sweet when she meets me, but only because I am helping her to have her own way. And I—my God, Minnie, I sit in the office and listen for her step outside!"

He moved a little and held out the paper in the candle-light.

"'It will please Americans to know,'" he read, "'that with the exception of the Venetian lace robe sent by the bridegroom's mother, all of Miss Patricia Jennings' elaborate trousseau is being made in America.

"'Prince Oskar and his suite, according to present arrangements, will sail from Naples early in March, and the wedding date, although not yet definitely fixed, will probably be the first week in April. The wedding party will include—'"

He stopped there, and looked at me, trying to smile.

"I knew it all before," he said, "but there's something inevitable about print. I guess I hadn't realized it."

He had the same look of wretchedness he'd had the first night I saw him—a hungry look—and I couldn't help it; I went over to him and patted him on the head like a little boy. I was only the spring-house girl, but I was older than he was, and he needed somebody to comfort him.

"I can't think of anything to say that will help any," I said, "unless it's what you wrote yourself on the blackboard down in the hall, 'Keep busy and you'll keep happy.'"

He reached up for my hand, and rough and red as it was—having been in the spring for so many years—he kissed it.

"Good for you, Minnie!" he said. "You're rational, and for a day or so I haven't been. That's right, KEEP BUSY. I'll do it." He got up and put his hands on my shoulders. "Good old pal, when you see me going around as if all the devils of hell were tormenting me, just come up and say that to me, will you?"

I promised, and he opened the door, candle in hand, and smiling.

"I'm a thousand per cent. better already," he said. "I just needed to tell somebody, I think. I dare say I've made a lot more fuss than it really deserves."

At the far end of the hall, a girl came out of one room, and carrying a candle, went across to another. It was Miss Patty, going to bid her father good night. When I left, he was still staring down the hall after her, his candle dripping wax on the floor, and his face white. I guess he hadn't overstated his case.

CHAPTER XXV

THE FIRST FRUITS

By Friday of that week you would hardly have known any of them. The fat ones were thinner and the thin ones fatter, and Miss Julia Summers could put her whole hand inside her belt.

And they were pleasant. They'd sit down to a supper of ham and eggs and apple sauce, and yell for more apple sauce, and every evening in the billiard room they got up two weighing pools, one for the ones who wanted to reduce, and one for the people who wanted to gain. Everybody put in a dollar, and at gymnasium hour the next morning the ones who'd gained or lost the most won the pool. Mr. Thoburn won the losing pool on Thursday and Friday—he didn't want to lose weight, but he was compelled to under the circumstances. And I think worry helped him to it.

They fussed some still about sleeping with the windows open, especially the bald-headed men. However, the bishop, who had been bald for thirty years, was getting a fine down all over the top of his head, and this encouraged the rest. The bishop says it is nature's instinct to protect itself from cold—all animals have fur, and heavier fur in winter—and he believed that it was the ultimate cure for baldness. Men lose their hair on top, he said, because they wear hats, and so don't need it. But let the top of the head need protection, and lo, hair comes there. Although, as Mr. Thoburn said, his nose was always cold in winter, and nature never did anything for IT.

Mr. von Inwald was still there, and not troubling himself to be agreeable to any but the Jennings family. He and Mr. Pierce carefully avoided each other, but I knew well enough that only policy kept them apart. Both of them, you see, were working for something.

Miss Cobb came to the spring-house early Friday morning, and from the way she came in and shut the door I knew she had something on her mind. She walked over to where I was polishing the brass railing around the spring—it had been the habit of years, and not easy to break—and stood looking at me and breathing hard.

"Minnie," she exclaimed, "I have found the thief!"

"Lord have mercy!" I said, and dropped the brass polish.

"I have found the thief!" she repeated firmly. "Minnie, our sins always find us out."

"I guess they do," I said shakily, and sat down on the steps to the spring. "Oh, Miss Cobb, if only he would use a little bit of sense!"

"He?" she said. "HE nothing! It's that Summers woman I'm talking about, Minnie. I knew that woman wasn't what she ought to be the minute I set eyes on her."

"The Summers woman!" I repeated.

Miss Cobb leaned over the railing and shook a finger in my face.

"The Summers woman," she said. "One of the chambermaids found my—my PROTECTORS hanging in the creature's closet!"

I couldn't speak. There had been so much happening that I'd clean forgotten Miss Cobb and her woolen tights. And now to have them come back like this and hang themselves around my neck, so to speak—it was too much.

"Per—perhaps they're hers," I said weakly after a minute.

"Stuff and nonsense!" declared Miss Cobb. "Don't you think I know my own, with L. C. in white cotton on the band, and my own darning in the knee where I slipped on the ice? And more than that, Minnie, where those tights are, my letters are!"

I glanced at the pantry, where her letters were hidden on the upper shelf. The door was closed.

"But—but what would she want with the letters?" I asked, with my teeth fairly hitting together. Miss Cobb pushed her forefinger into my shoulder.

"To blackmail me," she said, in a tragic voice, "or perhaps to publish. I've often thought of that myself—they're so beautiful. Letters from a life insurance agent to his lady-love—interesting, you know, and alliterative. As for that woman—!"

"What woman!" said Miss Summers' voice from behind us. We jumped and turned. "I always save myself trouble, so if by any chance you are discussing me—"

"As it happens," Miss Cobb said, glaring at her, "I WAS discussing you."

"Fine!" said Miss Julia. "I love to talk about myself."

"I doubt if it's an edifying subject," Miss Cobb snapped.

Miss Julia looked at her and smiled.

"Perhaps not," she said, "but interesting. Don't put yourself out to be friendly to me, Miss Cobb, if you don't feel like it."

"Are you going to return my letters?" Miss Cobb demanded.

"Your letters?"

"My letters—that you took out of my room!"

"Look here," Miss Julia said, still in a good humor, "don't you suppose I've got letters of my own, without bothering with another woman's?"

"Perhaps," Miss Cobb replied in triumph, "perhaps you will say that you don't know anything of my—of my black woolen protectors?"

"Never heard of them!" said Miss Summers. "What are they?" And then she caught my eye, and I guess I looked stricken. "Oh!" she said.

"Miss Cobb was robbed the other night," I explained, as quietly as I could. "Somebody went into her room and took a bundle of letters."

"Letters!" Miss Summers straightened and looked at me.

"And my woolen tights," said Miss Cobb indignantly, "with all this cold weather and military walks, and having to sit two hours a day by an open window! And I'll tell you this, Miss Summers, your dog got in my room that night, and while I have no suspicions, the chambermaid found my—er—missing garment this morning in your closet!"

"I don't believe," Miss Julia said, looking hard at me, "that Arabella would steal anything so—er—grotesque! Do you mean to say," she added slowly, "that nothing was taken from that room but the—lingerie and a bundle of letters?"

"Exactly," said Miss Cobb, "and I'd thank you for the letters."

"The letters!" Miss Julia retorted. "I've never been in your room. I haven't got the letters. I've never seen them." Then a light dawned in her face. "I—oh, it's the funniest ever!"

And with that she threw her head back and laughed until the tears rolled down her cheeks and she held her side.

"Screaming!" she gasped. "It's screaming! But, oh, Minnie, to have seen your face!"

Miss Cobb swept to the door and turned in a fury.

"I do not think it is funny," she stormed, "and I shall report to Mr. Carter at once what I have discovered."

She banged out, and Miss Julia put her head on a card-table and writhed with joy. "To have seen your face, Minnie!" she panted, wiping her eyes. "To have thought you had Dick Carter's letters, that I keep rolled in asbestos, and then to have opened them and found they were to Miss Cobb!"

"Be as happy as you like," I snapped, "but you are barking up the wrong tree. I don't know anything about any letters and as far as that goes, do you think I've lived here fourteen years to get into the wrong room at night? If I'd wanted to get into your room, I'd have found your room, not Miss Cobb's."

She sat up and pulled her hat straight, looking me right in the eye.

"If you'll recall," she said, "I came into the spring-house, and Arabella pulled that—garment of Miss Cobb's off a table. It was early—nobody was out yet. You were alone, Minnie, or no," she said suddenly, "you were not alone. Minnie, WHO was in the pantry?"

"What has that to do with it?" I managed, with my feet as cold as stone.

She got up and buttoned her sweater.

"Don't trouble to lie," she said. "I can see through a stone wall as well as most people. Whoever got those letters thought they were stealing mine, and there are only two people who would try to steal my letters; one is Dick Carter, and the other is his brother-in-law. It wasn't Sam in the pantry—he came in just after with his little snip of a wife."

"Well?" I managed.

But she was smiling again, not so pleasantly.

"I might have known it!" she said. "What a fool I've been, Minnie, and how clever you are under that red thatch of yours! Dicky can not appear as long as I am here, and Pierce takes his place, and I help to keep the secret and to play the game! Well, I can appreciate a joke on myself as well as most people, but—Minnie, Minnie, think of that guilty wretch of a Dicky Carter shaking in the pantry!"

"I don't know what you are talking about," I said, but she only winked and went to the door.

"Don't take it too much to heart," she advised. "Too much loyalty is a vice, not a virtue. And another piece of advice, Minnie—when I find Dicky Carter, stand from under; something will fall."

They had charades during the rest hour that afternoon, the overweights headed by the bishop, against the underweights headed by Mr. Moody. They selected their words from one of Horace Fletcher's books, and as Mr. Pierce wasn't either over or underweight, they asked him to be referee.

Oh, they were crazy about him by that time. It was "Mr. Carter" here and "dear Mr. Carter" there, with the women knitting him neckties and the men coming up to be bullied and asking for more.

And he kept the upper hand, too, once he got it. It was that day, I think, that he sent Senator Biggs up to make his bed again, and nobody in the place will ever forget how he made old Mr. Jennings hang his gymnasium suit up three times before it was done properly. The old man was mad enough at the time, but inside of twenty minutes he was offering Mr. Pierce the cigar he'd won in the wood-chopping contest.

But if Mr. Pierce was making a hit with the guests, he wasn't so popular with the Van Alstynes or the Carters. The night the cigar stand was closed Mr. Sam came to me and leaned over the counter.

"Put the key in a drawer," he said. "I can slip down here after the lights are out and get a smoke."

"Can't do it, Mr. Van Alstyne," I said. "Got positive orders."

"That doesn't include me." He was still perfectly good-humored.

"Sorry," I said. "Have to have a written order from Mr. Pierce."

He put a silver dollar on the desk between us and looked at me over it.

"Will that open the case?" he asked. But I shook my head.

"Well, I'll be hanged! What the devil sort of order did he give you?"

"He said," I repeated, "that I'd be coaxed and probably bribed to open the cigar case, and that you'd probably be the first one to do it, but I was to stick firm; you've been smoking too much, and your nerves are going."

"Insolent young puppy!" he exclaimed angrily, and stamped away.

So that I was not surprised when on that night, Friday, I was told to be at the shelter-house at ten o'clock for a protest meeting. Mrs. Sam told me.

"Something has to be done," she said. "I don't intend to stand much more. Nobody has the right to say when I shall eat or what. If I want to eat fried shoe leather, that's my affair."

We met at ten o'clock at the shelter-house, everybody having gone to bed—Miss Patty, the Van Alstynes and myself. The Dickys were on good terms again, for a wonder, and when we went in they were in front of the fire, she on a box and he at her feet, with his head buried in her lap. He didn't even look up when we entered.

"They're here, Dicky," she said.

"All right!" he answered in a smothered voice. "How many of 'em?"

"Four," she said, and kissed the tip of his ear.

"For goodness sake, Dick!" Mrs. Sam snapped in a disgusted tone, "stop that spooning and get us something to sit on."

"Help yourself," he replied, still from his wife's lap, "and don't be jealous, sis. If the sight of married happiness upsets you, go away. Go away, anyhow."

Mr. Sam came over and jerked him into a sitting position. "Either you'll sit up and take part in this discussion," he said angrily, "or you'll go out in the snow until it's over."

Mr. Dick leaned over and kissed his wife's hand.

"A cruel fate is separating us," he explained, "but try to endure it until I return. I'll be on the other side of the fireplace."

Miss Patty came to the fire and stood warming her hands. I saw her sister watching her.

"What's wrong with you, Pat?" she asked. "Oskar not behaving?"

"Don't be silly," Miss Patty said. "I'm all right."

"She's worked to death," Mrs. Sam put in. "Look at all of us. I'll tell you I'm so tired these nights that by nine o'clock I'm asleep on my feet."

"I'm tired to death, but I don't sleep," Miss Patty said. "I—I don't know why."

"I do," her sister said. "If you weren't so haughty, Pat, and would just own up that you're sick of your bargain—"

"Dolly!" Miss Patty got red and then white.

"Oh, all right," Mrs. Dicky said, and shrugged her shoulders. "Only, I hate to see you make an idiot of yourself, when I'm so happy."

Mr. Dick made a move at that to go across the fireplace to her, but Mr. Sam pushed him back where he was.

"You stay right there," he said. "Here's Pierce now."

He came in smiling, and as he stood inside the door, brushing the snow off, it was queer to see how his eyes went around the circle until he'd found Miss Patty and stopped at her.

Nobody answered his smile, and he came over to the fire beside Miss Patty.

"Great night!" he said, looking down at her. "There's something invigorating in just breathing that wind."

"Do you think so?" Mrs. Sam said disagreeably. "Of course, we haven't all got your shoulders."

"That's so," he answered, turning to her. "I said you women should not come so far. We could have met in my sitting-room."

"You forget one thing," Mr. Dick put in disagreeably, "and that is that this meeting concerns me, and I can not very well go to YOUR sitting-room."

"Fact," said Mr. Pierce, "I'd forgotten about you for the moment."

"You generally do," Mr. Dick retorted. "If you want the truth, Pierce, I'm about tired of your high-handed methods."

Mr. Pierce set his jaw and looked down at him.

"Why? I've saved the place, haven't I? Why, look here," he said, and pulled out a couple of letters, "these are the first fruits of those that weep—in other words, per aspera ad astra! Two new guests coming the last of the week—want to be put in training!"

Well, that was an argument nobody could find fault with, but their grievance was about themselves and they couldn't forgive him. They turned on him in the most heartless way—even Miss Patty—and demanded that he give them special privileges—breakfast when they wanted it, and Mr. Sam the key to the bar. And he stood firm, as he had that day in the lobby, and let the storm beat around him, looking mostly at Miss Patty. It was more than I could bear.

"Shame on all of you!" I said. "He's done what he promised he'd do, and more. If he did what he ought, he'd leave this minute, and let you find out for yourself what it is to drive thirty-odd different stomachs and the same number of bad dispositions in one direction."

"You are perfectly right, Minnie," Miss Patty said. "We're beastly, all of us, and I'm sorry." She went over and held out her hand to him. "You've done the impossible," she told him. He beamed.

"Your approval means more than anything," he said, holding her hand. Mrs. Dick sat up and opened her eyes wide.

"Speaking of Oskar," she began, and then stopped, staring past her sister, toward the door.

We all turned, and there, blinking in the light, was Miss Summers.

CHAPTER XXVI

OVER THE FENCE IS OUT

"WELL!" she said, and stood staring. Then she smiled—I guess our faces were funny.

"May I come in?" she asked, and without waiting she came in and closed the door. "You DO look cozy!" she said, and shook herself free of snow.

Mr. Dick had turned white. He got up with his eyes on her, and twice he opened his mouth and couldn't speak. He backed, still watching her, to his wife, and stood in front of her, as if to protect her.

Mr. Sam got his voice first.

"B—bad night for a walk," he said.

"Frightful!" she said. "I've been buried to my knees. May I sit down?" To those of us who knew, her easy manner had something horrible in it.

"Sorry there are no chairs, Julia," Mr. Pierce said. "Sit on the cot, won't you?"

"Who IS it?" Mrs. Dick asked from, as you may say, her eclipse. She and Miss Summers were the only calm ones in the room.

"I—I don't know," Mr. Dick stammered, but the next moment Miss Julia, from the cot, looked across at him and grinned.

"Well, Dicky!" she said. "Who'd have thought it!"

"You said you didn't know her!" his wife said from behind him.

"Who'd have thought wha—what?" he asked with bravado.

"All this!" Miss Julia waved her hand around the room, with its bare walls, and blankets over the windows to keep the light in and the cold out, and the circle of us sitting around on sand boxes from the links and lawn rollers. "To find you here, all snug in your own home, with your household gods and a wife." Nobody could think of anything to say. "That is," she went on, "I believe there is a wife. Good heavens, Dicky, it isn't Minnie?"

He stepped aside at that, disclosing Mrs. Dick on her box, with her childish eyes wide open.

"There—there IS a wife, Julia," he said. "This is her—she."

Well, she'd come out to make mischief—it was written all over her when she came in the door, but when Mr. Dick presented his wife, frightened as he was and still proud of her, and Mrs. Dick smiled in her pretty way, Miss Summers just walked across and looked down at her with a queer look on her face.

I shut my eyes and waited for the crash, but nothing came, and when I opened them again there were the two women holding hands and Miss Summers smiling a sort of crooked grin at Mr. Dick.

"I ought to be very angry with your husband," she said. "I—well, I never expected him to marry without my being among those present. But since he has done it—! Dick, you wretched boy, you took advantage of my being laid up with the mumps!"

"Mumps!" Mrs. Dick said. "Why, he has just had them himself!" She looked around the circle suspiciously, and every one of us looked as guilty as if he had been caught with the mumps concealed around him somewhere.

"I didn't have real mumps," Mr. Dick explained. "It was only—er—a swelling."

"You SAID it was mumps, and even now you hate pickles!"

Mr. Pierce had edged over to Miss Summers and patted her shoulder.

"Be a good sport, Julia," he whispered.

She threw off his hand.

"I'm being an idiot!" she said angrily. "Dick's an ass, and he's treated me like a villain, but look at that baby! It will be twenty years before she has to worry about her weight."

"I never cared for pickles," Mr. Dick was saying with dignity. "The doctor said—"

"I think we'd better be going." Miss Patty got up and gathered up her cloak. But if she meant to break up the party Miss Summers was not ready.

"If you don't mind," she said, "I'll stay. I'm frozen, and I've got to go home and sleep with my window up. You're lucky," she went on to the Dickys. "I dare say the air in here would scare us under a microscope, but at least it is warm."

The Van Alstynes made a move to go, but Mr. Dicky frantically gestured to them not to leave him alone, and Mrs. Sam sat down again sulkily. Mr. Pierce picked up his cap.

"I'll take you back," he said to Miss Patty, and his face was fairly glowing. But Miss Patty slipped her arm through mine.

"Come, Minnie, Mr. Pierce is going to take us," she said.

"I'd—I'd rather go alone," I said.

"Nonsense."

"I'm not ready. I've got to gather up these dishes," I objected.

Out of the corner of my eye I could see the glow dying out of Mr. Pierce's face. But Miss Patty took my arm and led me to the door.

"Let them gather up their own dishes," she said. "Dolly, you ought to be ashamed to let Minnie slave for you the way she does. Good night, everybody."

I did my best to leave them alone on the way back, but Miss Patty stuck close to my heels. It was snowing, and the going was slow.

For the first five minutes she only spoke once.

"And so Miss Summers and Dicky Carter are old friends!"

"It appears so," Mr. Pierce said.

"She's rather magnanimous, under the circumstances," Miss Patty remarked demurely.

"Under what circumstances?"

I heard her laugh a little, behind me.

"Never mind," she said. "You needn't tell me anything you don't care to. But what a stew you must all have been in!"

There was a minute's silence behind me, and then Mr. Pierce laughed too.

"Stew!" he said. "For the last few days I've been either paralyzed with fright or electrified into wild bursts of mendacity. And I'm not naturally a liar."

"Really!" she retorted. "What an actor you are!"

They laughed together at that, and I gained a little on them. At the corner where the path skirted the deer park and turned toward the house I lost them altogether and I floundered on alone. But I had not gone twenty feet when I stopped suddenly. About fifty yards ahead a lantern was coming toward me through the snow, and I could hear a man's voice, breathless and gasping.

"Set it down," it said. "The damned thing must be filled with lead." It sounded like Thoburn.

"It's the snow," another voice replied, Mr. von Inwald's. "I told you it would take two trips."

"Yes," Thoburn retorted, breathing in groans. "Stay up all night to get the blamed stuff here, and then get up at dawn for a cold bath and a twenty-mile walk and an apple for breakfast. Ugh, my shoulder is dislocated."

I turned and flew back to Miss Patty and Pierce. They had stopped in the shelter of the fence corner and Mr. Pierce was on his knees in front of her! I was so astounded that I forgot for the moment what had brought me.

"Just a second," he was saying. "It's ice on the heel."

"Please get up off your knees, you'll take cold."

"Never had a cold. I'll scrape it off with my knife. Why don't you wear overshoes?"

"I never have a cold!" she retorted. "Why, Minnie, is that you?"

"Quick," I panted. "Thoburn and Mr. von Inwald coming—basket—lantern—warn the shelter-house!"

"Great Scott!" Mr. Pierce said. "Here, you girls crawl over the fence: you'll be hidden there. I'll run back and warn them."

The lantern was swinging again. Mr. Thoburn's grumbling came to us through the snow, monotonous and steady.

"I can't climb the fence!" Miss Patty said pitifully. But Mr. Pierce had gone.

I reached my basket through the bars and climbed the fence in a hurry. Miss Patty had got almost to the top and was standing there on one snow-covered rail, staring across at me through the darkness.

"I can't, Minnie," she whispered hopelessly. "I never could climb a fence, and in this skirt—!"

"Quick!" I said in a low tone. The lantern was very close. "Put your leg over."

She did, and sat there looking down at me like a scared baby.

"Now the other."

"I—I can't!" she whispered. "If I put them both over I'll fall."

"Hurry!"

With a little grunt she put the other foot over, sat a minute with agony in her face and her arms out, then she slid off with a squeal and brought up in a sitting position inside the fence corner. I dropped beside her.

"What was that noise?" said Mr. Thoburn, almost upon us. "Something's moving inside that fence corner."

"It's them deers," Mike's voice this time. We could make out the three figures. "Darned nuisance, them deers is. They'd have been shot long ago if the spring-house girl hadn't objected. She thinks she's the whole cheese around here."

"Set it down again," Mr. von Inwald panted. We heard the rattle of bottles as they put down the basket, and the next instant Thoburn's fat hand was resting on the rail of the fence over our heads. I could feel Miss Patty trembling beside me.

But he didn't look over. He stood there resting, breathing hard, and swearing at the weather, while Mike waited, in surly silence, and the von Inwald cursed in German.

After my heart had been beating in my ears for about three years the fat hand moved, and I heard the rattle of glass again and Thoburn's groan as he bent over his half of the load.

"'Come on, my partners in distress, My comrades through this wilderness,'"

he said, and the others grunted and started on.

When they had disappeared in the snow we got out of our cramped position and prepared to scurry home. I climbed the fence and looked after them. "Humph!" I said, "I guess that basket isn't for the hungry poor. I'd give a good bit to know—" Then I turned and looked for Miss Patty. She was flat on the snow, crawling between the two lower rails of the fence.

"Have you no shame?" I demanded.

She looked up at me with her head and half her long sealskin coat through the fence.

"None," she said pitifully. "Minnie, I'm stuck perfectly tight!"

"You ought to be left as you are," I said, jerking at her, "for people to come"—jerk—"to-morrow to look at"—jerk. She came through at that, and we lay together in the snow and like to burst a rib laughing.

"You'll never be a princess, Miss Patty," I declared. "You're too lowly minded."

She sat up suddenly and straightened her sealskin cap on her head.

"I wish," she said unpleasantly, "I wish you wouldn't always drag in disagreeable things, Minnie!"

And she was sulky all the way to the house.

Miss Summers came to my room that night as I was putting my hot-water bottle to bed, in a baby-blue silk wrapper with a band of fur around the low neck—Miss Summers, of course, not the hot-water bottle.

"Well!" she said, sitting down on the foot of the bed and staring at me. "Well, young woman, for a person who has never been farther away than Finleyville you do pretty well!"

"Do what?" I asked, with the covers up to my chin.

"Do what, Miss Innocence!" she said mockingly. "You're the only red-haired woman I ever saw who didn't look as sophisticated as the devil. I'll tell you one thing, though." She reached down into the pocket of her dressing-gown and brought up a cigarette and a match. "You never had me fooled for a minute!" She looked at me over the match.

I lay and stared back.

"And another thing," she said. "I never had any real intention of marrying Dicky Carter and raising a baby sanatorium. I wouldn't have the face to ask Arabella to live here."

"I'm glad you feel that way, Miss Summers," I said. "I've gone through a lot; I'm an old woman in the last two weeks. My hair's falling from its having to stand up on end half the time."

She leaned over and put her cigarette on the back of my celluloid mirror, and then suddenly she threw back her head and laughed.

"Minnie!" she said, between fits, "Minnie! As long as I live I'll never forget that wretched boy's face! And the sand boxes! And the blankets over the windows! And the tarpaulin over the rafters! And Mr. Van Alstyne sitting on the lawnmower! I'd rather have had my minute in that doorway than fifty thousand dollars!"

"If you had had to carry out all those things—" I began, but she checked me.

"Listen!" she said. "Somebody with brains has got to take you young people in hand. You're not able to look after yourselves. I'm fond of Alan Pierce, for one thing, and I don't care to see a sanatorium that might have been the child of my solicitude kidnaped and reared as a summer hotel by Papa Thoburn. A good fat man is very, very good, Minnie, but when he is bad he is horrid."

"It's too late," I objected feebly. "He can't get it now."

"Can't he!" She got up and yawned, stretching. "Well, I'll lay you ten to one that if we don't get busy he'll have the house empty in thirty-six hours, and a bill of sale on it in as many days."

The celluloid mirror blazed up at that minute, and she poured the contents of my water-pitcher over the dresser. For the next hour, while I was emptying water out of the bureau drawers and hanging up my clothes to dry, she told me what she knew of Thoburn's scheme, and it turned me cold.

But I went to bed finally. Just as I was dozing off, somebody opened my door, and I heard a curious scraping along the floor. I turned on the light, and there was Arabella, half-dragging and half-carrying a solid silver hand-mirror with a card on it: "To Minnie, to replace the one that blew up. J. S."

CHAPTER XXVII

A CUPBOARD FULL OF RYE

Doctor Barnes came to me at the news stand the next morning before gymnasium.

"Well," he said, "you look as busy as a dog with fleas. Have you heard the glad tidings?"

"What?" I asked without much spirit. "I've heard considerable tidings lately, and not much of it has cheered me up any."

He leaned over and ran his fingers up through his hair.

"You know, Miss Minnie," he said, "somebody ought kindly to kill our friend Thoburn, or he'll come to a bad end."

"Shall I do it, or will you?" I said, filling up the chewing-gum jar. Mr. Pierce had taken away the candy case.

Doctor Barnes glanced around to see if there was any one near, and leaned farther over.

"The cupboard isn't empty now!" he said. "Not for nothing did I spend part of the night in the Dicky-bird's nest! By the way, did you ever hear that touching story about little Sally walking up and laying an egg?—I see you have. What do you think is in the cupboard?"

"I know about it," I said shortly. "Liquor—in a case labeled 'Books—breakable.'"

"'Sing a song of sixpence, a cupboard full of rye!'" he said. "Almost a goal! But not ONLY liquors, my little friend. Champagne—cases of it—caviar, canned grouse with truffles, lobster, cheeses, fine cigars, everything you could think of, erotic, exotic and narcotic. An orgy in cans and bottles, a bacchanalian revel: a cupboard full of indigestion, joy, forgetfulness and katzenjammer. Oh, my suffering palate, to have to leave it all without one sniff, one sip, one nibble!"

"He's wasting his money," I said. "They're all crazy about the simple life."

He looked around and, seeing no one in the lobby, reached over and took one of my hands.

"Strange," he said, looking at it. "No webs, and yet it's been an amphibious little creature most of its life. My dear girl, our friend Thoburn is a rascal, but he is also a student of mankind and a philosopher. Gee," he said, "think of a woman fighting her way alone through the world with a bit of a fist like that!"

I jerked my hand away.

"It's like this, my dear," he said. "Human nature's a curious thing. It's human nature, for instance, for me to be crazy about you, when you're as hands-offish as a curly porcupine. And it is human nature, by the same token, to like to be bullied, especially about health, and to respect and admire the fellow who does the bullying. That's why we were crazy about Roosevelt, and that's why Pierce is trailing his kingly robes over them while they lie on their faces and eat dirt—and stewed fruit."

He reached for my hand again, but I put it behind me.

"But alas," he said, "there is another side to human nature, and our friend Thoburn has not kept a summer hotel for nothing. It is notoriously weak, especially as to stomach. You may feed 'em prunes and whole-wheat bread and apple sauce, and after a while they'll forget the fat days, and remember only the lean and hungry ones. But let some student of human nature at the proper moment introduce just one fat day, one feast, one revel—"

"Talk English," I said sharply.

"Don't break in on my flights of fancy," he objected. "If you want the truth, Thoburn is going to have a party—a forbidden feast. He's going to rouse again the sleeping dogs of appetite, and send them ravening back to the Plaza, to Sherry's and Del's and the little Italian restaurants on Sixth Avenue. He's going to take them up on a high mountain and show them the wines and delicatessen of the earth, and then ask them if they're going to be bullied into eating boiled beef and cabbage."

"Then I don't care how soon he does it," I said despondently. "I'd rather die quickly than by inches."

"Die!" he said. "Not a bit of it. Remember, our friend Pierce is also a student of human nature. He's thinking it out now in the cold plunge, and I miss my guess if Thoburn's sky-rocket hasn't got a stick that'll come back and hit him on the head."

He had been playing with one of the chewing-gum jars, and when he had gone I shoved it back into its place. It was by the merest chance that I glanced at it, and I saw that he had slipped a small white box inside. I knew I was being a silly old fool, but my heart beat fast when I took it out and looked at it. On the lid was written "For a good girl," and inside lay the red puffs from Mrs. Yost's window down in Finleyville. Just under them was an envelope. I could scarcely see to open it.

"Dearest Minnie," the note inside said, "I had them matched to my own thatch, and I think they'll match yours. And since, in the words of the great Herbert Spencer, things that match the same thing match each other—! What do you say?—Barnes."

"P. S.—I love you. I feel like a damn fool saying it, but heaven knows it's true."

"P. P. S.—Still love you. It's easier the second time."

"N. B.—I love you—got the habit now and can't stop writing it.—B."

Well, I had to keep calm and attend to business, but I was seething inside like a Seidlitz powder. Every few minutes I'd reread the letter under the edge of the stand, and the more I read it the more excited I got. When a woman's gone past thirty before she gets her first love-letter, she isn't sure whether to thank providence or the man, but she's pretty sure to make a fool of herself.

Thoburn came to the news stand on his way out with the ice-cutting gang to the pond.

"Last call to the dining-car, Minnie," he said. "'Will you—won't you—will you—won't you—will you join the dance?'"

"I haven't any reason for changing my plans," I retorted. "I promised the old doctor to stick by the place, and I'm sticking."

"As the man said when he sat down on the flypaper. You're going by your heart, Minnie, and not by your head, and in this toss, heads win."

But with my new puffs on the back of my head, and my letter in my pocket, I wasn't easy to discourage. Thoburn shouldered his pick and, headed by Doctor Barnes, the ice-cutters started out in single file. As they passed the news stand Doctor Barnes glanced at me, and my heart almost stopped.

"Do they—is it a match?" he asked, with his eyes on mine.

I couldn't speak, but I nodded "yes," and all that afternoon I could see the wonderful smile that lit up his face as he went out. It made him almost good-looking. Oh, there's nothing like love, especially if you've waited long enough to be hungry for it, and not spoiled your taste for it by a bite here and a piece of a heart there, beforehand, so to speak.

Miss Cobb stopped at the news stand on her way to the gymnasium. She was a homely woman at any time, and in her bloomers she looked like a soup-bone. Under ordinary circumstances she'd have seen the puffs from the staircase and have asked what they cost and told me they didn't match, in one breath. But she had something else on her mind. She padded over to the counter in her gym shoes, and for once she'd forgotten her legs.

"May I speak to you, Minnie?" she asked.

"You mostly do," I said. "There isn't a new rule about speaking, is there?"

"This is important, Minnie," she said, rolling her eyes around as she always did when she was excited. "I'm in such a state of ex—I see you bought the puffs! Perhaps you will lend them to me if we arrange for a country dance."

"They don't match," I objected. "They—they wouldn't look natural, Miss Cobb."

"They don't look natural on you, either. Do you suppose anybody believes that the Lord sent you hair in seventeen rows of pipes, so that, red as it is, it looks like an instantaneous water-heater?"

"I'm not lending them," I said firmly. It would have been like lending an engagement ring, to my mind. Miss Cobb was not offended. She went at once to what had brought her, and bent over the counter.

"Where's the Summers woman?" she asked.

"In the gym. She's made herself a new gym suit out of her polka dotted silk, and she looks lovely."

"Humph!" retorted Miss Cobb. "Minnie, you love Miss Jennings almost like a daughter, don't you?"

"Like a sister, Miss Cobb," I said. "I'm not feeble yet."

"Well, you wouldn't want to see her deceived."

"I wouldn't have it," I answered.

"Then what do you call this?" She put a small package on the counter, and stared at me over it. "There's treachery here, black treachery." She pointed one long thin forefinger at the bundle.

"What is it? A bomb?" I asked, stepping back. More than once it had occurred to me that having royalty around sometimes meant dynamite. Miss Cobb showed her teeth.

"Yes, a bomb," she said. "Minnie, since that creature took my letters and my er—protectors, I have suspected her. Now listen. Yesterday I went over the letters and I missed one that beautiful one in verse, beginning, 'Oh, creature of the slender form and face!' Minnie, it had disappeared—melted away."

"I'm not surprised," I said.

"And so, last night, when the Summers woman was out, goodness knows where, Blanche Moody and I went through her room. We did not find my precious missive from Mr. Jones, but we did find these, Minnie, tied around with a pink silk stocking."

"Heavens!" I said, mockingly. "Not a pink silk!"

"Pink," she repeated solemnly. "Minnie, I have felt it all along. Mr. Oskar von Inwald is the prince himself."

"No!"

"Yes. And more than that, he is making desperate love to Miss Summers. Three of those letters were written in one day! Why, even Mr. Jones—"

"The wretch!" I cried. I was suddenly savage. I wanted to take Mr. von Inwald by the throat and choke him until his lying tongue was black, to put the letters where Miss Patty could never see them. I wanted—I had to stop to sell Senator Biggs some chewing-gum, and when he had gone, Miss Cobb was reaching out for the bundle. I snatched it from her.

"Give me those letters instantly," she cried shrilly. But I marched from behind the counter and over to the fireplace.

"Never," I said, and put the package on the log. When they were safely blazing, I turned and looked at Miss Cobb.

"I'd put my hand right beside those letters to save Miss Patty a heartache," I said, "and you know it."

"You're a fool." She was raging. "You'll let her marry him and have the heartaches afterward."

"She won't marry him," I snapped, and walked away with my chin up, leaving her staring.

But I wasn't so sure as I pretended to be. Mr. von Inwald and Mr. Jennings had been closeted together most of the morning, and Mr. von Inwald was whistling as he started out for the military walk. It seemed as if the very thing that had given Mr. Pierce his chance to make good had improved Mr. Jennings' disposition enough to remove the last barrier to Miss Jennings' wedding with somebody else.

Well, what's one man's meat is another man's poison.

CHAPTER XXVIII

LOVE, LOVE, LOVE

Even if we hadn't known, we'd have guessed there was something in the air. There was an air of subdued excitement during the rest hour in the spring-house, and a good bit of whispering and laughing, in groups which would break up with faces as long as the moral law the moment they saw my eye on them.

They were planning a mutiny, as you may say, and I guess no sailors on a pirate ship were more afraid of the captain's fist than they were of Mr. Pierce's disapproval. He'd been smart enough to see that most of them, having bullied other people all their lives, liked the novelty of being bullied themselves. And now they were getting a new thrill by having a revolt. They were terribly worked up.

Miss Patty stayed after the others had gone, sitting in front of the empty fireplace in the same chair Mr. Pierce usually took, and keeping her back to me. When I'd finished folding the steamer rugs and putting them away, I went around and stood in front of her.

"Your eyes are red," I remarked.

"I've got a cold." She was very haughty.

"Your nose isn't red," I insisted. "And, anyhow, you say you never have a cold."

"I wish you would let me alone, Minnie." She turned her back to me. "I dare say I may have a cold if I wish."

"Do you know what they are saying here?" I demanded. "Do you know that Miss Cobb has found out in some way or other who Mr. von Inwald is? And that the four o'clock gossip edition says your father has given his consent and that you can go and buy a diadem or whatever you are going to wear, right off?"

"Well," she said, in a choked voice, with her back to me, "what of it? Didn't you and Mr. Pierce both do your best to bring it about?"

"Our what?" I couldn't believe my ears.

"You made father well. He's so p—pleasant he'll do anything except leave this awful place!"

"Well, of all the ungrateful people—" I began, and then Mr. Pierce came in. He had a curious way of stopping when he saw her, as if she just took the wind out of his sails, so to speak, and then of whipping off his hat, if anything with sails can wear a hat, and going up to her with his heart in his eyes. He always went straight to her and stopped suddenly about two feet away, trying to think of something ordinary to say. Because the extraordinary thing he wanted to say was always on the end of his tongue.

But this day he didn't light up when he saw her. He went through all the other motions, but his mouth was set in a straight line, and when he came close to her and looked down his eyes were hard.

It's been my experience of men that the younger they are the harder they take things and the more uncompromising they are. It takes a good many years and some pretty hard knocks to make people tolerant.

"I was looking for you," he said to her. "The bishop has just told me. There are no obstacles now."

"None," she said, looking up at him with wretchedness in her eyes, if he had only seen. "I am very happy."

"She was just saying," I said bitterly, "how grateful she was to both of us."

"I don't understand."

"It is not hard to understand," she said, smiling. I wanted to slap her. "Father was unreasonable because he was ill. You have made him well. I can never thank you enough."

But she rather overdid the joy part of it, and he leaned over and looked in her face.

"I think I'm stupid," he said. "I know I'm unhappy. But isn't that what I was to do—to make them well if I could?"

"How could anybody know—" she began angrily, and then stopped. "You have done even more," she said sweetly. "You've turned them into cherubims and seraphims. Butter wouldn't melt in their mouths. Ugh! How I hate amiability raised to the NTH power!"

He smiled. I think it was getting through his thick man's skull that she wasn't so happy as she should have been, and he was thrilled through and through.

"My amiability must be the reason you dislike me!" he suggested. They had both forgotten me.

"Do I dislike you?" she asked, raising her eyebrows. "I never really thought about it, but I'm sure I don't." She didn't look at him, she looked at me. She knew I knew she lied.

His smile faded.

"Well," he said, "speaking of disliking amiability, you don't hate yourself, I'm sure."

"You are wrong," she retorted, "I loathe myself." And she walked to the window. He took a step or two after her.

"Why do it at all?" he asked in a low tone. "You don't love him—you can't. And if it isn't love—" He remembered me suddenly and stopped.

"Please go on," she said sweetly from the window. "Do not mind Minnie. She is my conscience, anyhow. She is always scolding me; you might both scold in chorus."

"I wouldn't presume to scold."

"Then give me a little advice and look superior and righteous. I'm accustomed to that also."

"As long as you are in this mood, I can't give you anything but a very good day," he said angrily, and went toward the door. But when he had almost reached it he turned.

"I will say this," he said, "you have known for three days that Mr. Thoburn was going to have a supper to-night, and you didn't let us know. You must have known his purpose."

I guess I was as surprised as she was. I'd never suspected she knew.

She looked at him over her shoulder.

"Why shouldn't he have a supper?" she demanded angrily. "I'm starving—we're all starving for decent food. I'm kept here against my will. Why shouldn't I have one respectable meal? You with your wretched stewed fruits and whole-wheat breads! Ugh!"

"I'm sorry. Thoburn's idea, of course, is to make the guests discontented, so they will leave."

"Oh!" she said. She hadn't thought of that, and she flushed. "At least," she said, "you must give me credit for not trying to spoil Dick and Dolly's chance here."

"We are going to allow the party to go on," he said, still stiff and uncompromising. It would have been better if he'd accepted her bit of apology.

"How kind of you! I dare say he would have it, anyhow." She was sarcastic again.

"Probably. And you—will go?"

"Certainly."

"Even when the result—"

"Oh, don't preach!" she said, putting her hands to her ears. "If you and Minnie want to preach, why don't you preach at each other? Minnie talks 'love, love, love.' And you preach health and morality. You drive me crazy between you."

"Suppose," he said with a gleam in his eyes, "suppose I preach 'love, love, love!'"

She put her fingers in her ears again. "Say it to Minnie," she cried, and turned her back to him.

"Very well," he said. "Minnie, Miss Jennings refuses to listen, and there are some things I must say. Once again I am going to register a protest against her throwing herself away in a loveless marriage. I—I feel strongly on the subject, Minnie."

She half turned, as if to interrupt. Then she thought better of it and kept her fingers in her ears, her face flushed. But he had learned what he hoped—that she could hear him.

"You ask me why I feel so strongly, Minnie, and you are right to ask. Under ordinary circumstances, Minnie, any remark of mine on the subject would be ridiculous impertinence."

He stopped and eyed her back, but she did not move.

"It is impertinence under any circumstances, but consider the provocation. I see a young, beautiful and sensitive girl, marrying, frankly without love, a man whom I know to be unworthy, and you ask me to stand aside and allow it to happen!"

"Are you still preaching?" she asked coldly over her shoulder. "It must be a long sermon."

And then, knowing he had only a moment more, his voice changed and became deep and earnest. His hands, that were clutching a chair-back, took a stronger hold, so that the ends of the nails were white.

"You see, Minnie," he said, turning a little pale, "I—I love Miss Jennings myself. You have known it a long time, for you love her, too. It has come to the point that I measure the day by the hours when I can see her. She doesn't care for me; sometimes I think she hates me." He paused here, but Miss Patty didn't move. "I haven't anything to offer a woman except a clean life and the kind of love that a woman could be proud of. I have no title—"

Miss Patty suddenly took her fingers out of her ears and turned around. She was flushed and shaken, but she looked past him without blinking an eyelash to me.

"Dear me," she said, "the sermon must have been exciting, Minnie! You are quite trembly!"

And with that she picked up her muff and went out, with not a glance at him.

He looked at me.

"Well," he said, "THAT'S over. She's angry, Minnie, and she'll never forgive me."

"Stuff!" I snapped, "I notice she waited to hear it all, and no real woman ever hated a man for saying he loved her."

CHAPTER XXIX

A BIG NIGHT TO-NIGHT

I carried out the supper to the shelter-house as usual that night, but I might have saved myself the trouble. Mrs. Dicky was sitting on a box, with her hair in puffs and the folding card-table before her, and Mr. Dick was uncorking a bottle of champagne with a nail. There were two or three queer-smelling cans open on the table.

Mrs. Dick looked at my basket and turned up her nose.

"Put it anywhere, Minnie," she said loftily, "I dare say it doesn't contain anything reckless."

"Cold ham and egg salad," I said, setting it down with a slam. "Stewed prunes and boiled rice for dessert. If those cans taste as they smell, you'd better keep the basket to fall back on. Where'd you get THAT?" Mr. Dick looked at me over the bottle and winked. "In the next room," he said, "iced to the proper temperature, paid for by somebody else, and coming after a two-weeks' drought! Minnie, there isn't a shadow on my joy!"

"He'll miss it," I said. But Mr. Dick was pouring out three large tumblersful of the stuff, and he held one out to me.

"Miss it!" he exclaimed. "Hasn't he been out three times to-day, tapping his little CACHE? And didn't he bring out Moody and the senator and von Inwald this afternoon, and didn't they sit in the next room there from two to four, roaring songs and cracking bottles and jokes."

"Beasts!" Mrs. Dicky said savagely. "Two hours, and we daren't move!"

"Drink, pretty creature!" Mr. Dick said, motioning to my glass. "Don't be afraid of it, Minnie; it's food and drink."

"I don't like it," I said, sipping at it. "I'd rather have the spring water."

"You'll have to cultivate a taste for it," he explained. "You'll like the second half better."

I got it down somehow and started for the door. Mr. Dick came after me with something that smelled fishy on the end of a fork.

"Better eat something," he suggested. "That was considerable champagne, Minnie."

"Stuff and nonsense," I said. "I was tired and it has rested me. That's all, Mr. Dick."

"Sure?"

"Certainly," I said with dignity, "I'm really rested, Mr. Dick. And happy—I'm very happy, Mr. Dick."

"Perhaps I'd better close the door," he said. "The light may be seen—"

"You needn't close it until I've finished talking," I said. "I've done my best for you and yours, Mr. Dick. I hope you appreciate it. Night after night I've tramped out here through the snow, and lost sleep, and lied myself black in the face—you've no idea how I've had to lie, Mr. Dick."

"Come in and shut the door, Dick," Mrs. Dick called, "I'm freezing."

That made me mad.

"Exactly," I said, glaring at her through the doorway. "Exactly—I can wade through the snow, bringing you meals that you scorn—oh, yes, you scorn them. What did you do to the basket tonight? Look at it, lying there, neglected in a corner, with p—perfectly good ham and stewed fruit in it."

All of a sudden I felt terrible about the way they had treated the basket, and I sat down on the steps and began to cry. I remember that, and Mr. Dick sitting down beside me and putting his arm around me and calling me "good old Minnie," and for heaven's sake not to cry so loud. But I was past caring. I had a sort of recollection of his getting me to stand up, and our walking through about twenty-one miles of snow to the spring-house. When we got there he stood off in the twilight and looked at me.

"I'm sorry, Minnie," he said, "I never dreamed it would do that."

"Do what?"

"Nothing. You're sure you won't forget?"

"I never forget," I said. I had got up the steps by this time and was trying to figure why the spring-house door had two knobs.

I hadn't any idea what he meant.

"Remember," he said, very slowly, "Thoburn is going to have his party to-night instead of to-morrow. Tell Pierce that. To-night, not to-morrow." I was pretty well ashamed when I got in the spring-house and sat down in the dark. I kept saying over and over to myself, so I'd not forget, "tonight, not to-morrow," but I couldn't remember WHAT was to be to-night. I was sleepy, too, and my legs were cold and numb. I remember going into the pantry for a steamer rug, and sitting down there for a minute, with the rug around my knees before I started to the house. And that is all I DO remember.

I was wakened by a terrible hammering in the top of my head. I reached out for the glass of water that I always put beside my bed at night and I touched a door-knob instead. Then I realized that the knocking wasn't all in my head. There was a sort of steady movement of feet on the other side of the door, with people talking and laughing. And above it all rose the steady knock—knock of somebody beating on tin.

"Can't do it." It was the bishop's voice. "I am convinced that nothing but dynamite will open this tin of lobster."

"Just a moment, Bishop," Mr. Thoburn's voice and the clink of bottles, "I have a can opener somewhere. You'll find the sauce a la Newburg—"

"Here, somebody, a glass, quick! A bottle's broken!"

"Did anybody remember to bring salt and pepper?"

"DEAR Mr. Thoburn!" It sounded like Miss Cobb. "Think of thinking of all this!"

"The credit is not mine, dear lady," Mr. Thoburn said. "Where the deuce is that corkscrew? No, dear lady, man makes his own destiny, but his birth date remains beyond his control."

"Ladies and gentlemen," somebody said, "to Mr. Thoburn's birthday being beyond his control!"

There was the clink of glasses, but I had remembered what it had been that I was to remember. And now it was too late. I was trapped in the pantry of my spring-house and Mr. Pierce was probably asleep. I clutched my aching head and tried to think. I was roused by hearing somebody say that Miss Jennings had no glass, and by steps nearing the pantry. I had just time to slip the bolt.

"Pantry's locked!" said a voice.

"Drat that Minnie!" somebody else said. "The girl's a nuisance."

"Hush!" Miss Summers said. "She's probably in there now—taking down what we say and what we eat. Convicting us out of our own mouths."

I held my breath and the knob rattled. Then they found a glass for Miss Patty and forgot the pantry.

Under cover of the next burst of noises I tried the pantry window, but it was frozen shut. Nothing but a hammer would have loosened it. I began to dig at it with a wire hairpin, but I hadn't much hope.

The fun in the spring-house was getting fast and furious. Miss Summers was leaning against the pantry door and I judged that most of the men in the room were around her, as usual. I put my ear to the panel of the door, and I could pretty nearly see what was going on. They were toasting Mr. Thoburn, and getting hungrier every minute as the supper was put out on the card-tables.

"To the bottle!" somebody said. "In infancy, the milk bottle; in our prime, the wine bottle; in our dotage, the pill bottle."

Mr. von Inwald came over and stood beside Miss Summers, and I could hear every whisper.

"I have good news for you," she said in an undertone.

"Oh! And what?"

"Sh! You may recall," she said, "the series of notes, letters, epistles, with which you have been honoring me lately?"

"How could I forget? They were written in my heart's blood!"

"Indeed!" Her voice lifted its eyebrows, so to speak. "Well, somebody got in my room last night and stole I dare say a pint of your heart's blood. They're gone."

He was pretty well upset, as he might be, and she stood by and listened to the things he said, which, if they were as bad in English as they sounded in German, I wouldn't like to write down.

And when he cooled down and condensed, as you may say, into English, he said Miss Jennings must have seen the letters, for she would hardly speak to him. And Miss Summers said she hoped Miss Jennings had—she was too nice a girl to treat shamefully.

And after he had left her there alone, I heard a sort of scratching on the door behind Miss Summers' back, and then something being shoved under the door. I stooped down and picked it up. It was a key!

I struck a match, and I saw by the tag that it was the one to the old doctor's rooms. I knew right off what it meant. Mr. Pierce had gone to bed, or pretended to throw them off the track and Thoburn had locked him in! Thoburn hadn't taken any chances. He knew the influence Mr. Pierce had over them all, and he and his champagne and tin cans had to get in their work before Mr. Pierce had another chance at them.

I had no time to wonder how Miss Summers knew I was in the pantry. I tried the window again, but it wouldn't work. Somebody in the spring-house was shouting, "'Hot butter blue beans, please come to supper!'" and I could hear them crowding around the tables. I worked frantically with the hairpin, and just then two shadowy figures outside slipped around the corner of the building. It was Mr. Pierce and Doctor Barnes!

I darted back and put my ear to the door, but they did not come in at once. Mr. Thoburn made a speech, saying how happy he was that they were all well and able to go back to civilization again, where the broiled lobster flourished like a green bay tree and the prune and the cabbage were unknown.

There was loud applause, and then Senator Biggs cleared his throat.

"Ladies and gentlemen, distinguished fellow guests," he began, "I suggest a toast to the autocrat of Hope Springs. It is the only blot on the evening, that, owing to the exigencies of the occasion, he can not be with us. Securely fastened in his room, he is now sleeping the sleep that follows a stomach attuned to prunes, a mind attuned to rule."

"Eat, drink and be merry!" somebody said, "for to-morrow you diet!"

There was a swish and rustle, as if a woman got up in a hurry.

"Do you mean," said Miss Patty's clear voice, "that you have dared to lock Mr. Pier—Mr. Carter in his room?"

"My dear young lady," several of them began, but she didn't give them time.

"It is outrageous, infamous!" she stormed. I didn't need to see her to know how she looked.

"How DARE you! Suppose the building should catch fire!"

"Fire!" somebody said in a bewildered voice. "My dear young lady—"

"Don't 'my dear young lady' me," she said angrily. "Father, Bishop, will you stand for this? Why, he may jump out the window and hurt himself! Give me the key!"

Miss Julia's fingers were beating a tatoo behind her, as if she was afraid I might miss it.

"If he jumps out he probably will hurt himself. It is impossible to release him now, Miss Jennings, but if you insist we can have a mattress placed under the window."

"Thanks, Thoburn. It won't be necessary." The voice came from the door, and a hush fell on the party. I slipped my bolt and peeped out. Framed in the doorway was Mr. Pierce, with Doctor Barnes looking over his shoulder.

The people in the spring-house were abject. That's the only word for it. Craven, somebody suggested later, and they were that, too. They smiled sickly grins and tried to be defiant, and most of them tried to put down whatever they held in their hands and to look innocent. If you ever saw a boy when his school-teacher asks him what he has in his mouth, and multiply the boy thirty times in number and four times in size, you'll know how they looked.

Mr. Pierce never smiled. He wouldn't let them speak a word in defense or explanation. He simply lined them up as he did at gym, and sent them, one by one, to the corner with whatever they had in their hands. He made Mr. Jennings give up a bottle of anchovies that he'd stuffed in his pocket, and the bishop had to come over with a cheese.

And when it was all over, he held the door open and they went back to the house. They fairly ducked past him in the doorway, although he hadn't said a dozen words. It was a rout. The backbone of the rebellion was broken. I knew that never again would the military discipline of Hope Springs be threatened. Thoburn might as well pack and go. It was Mr. Pierce's day.

Mr. von Inwald was almost the last. He stood by, sneering, with an open bottle of olives in his hand, watching the others go out.

Mr. Pierce held the door open and eyed him.

"I'll trouble you to put that bottle with the others, in the corner," Mr. Pierce said sternly.

They stood glaring at each other angrily.

"And if I refuse?"

"You know the rules here. If you refuse, there is a hotel at Finleyville."

Mr. von Inwald glanced past Mr. Pierce to where Doctor Barnes stood behind him, with his cauliflower ear and his pugilist's shoulders. Then he looked at the bottle in his hand, and from it to Miss Patty, standing haughtily by.

"I have borne much for you, Patricia," he said, "but I refuse to be bullied any longer. I shall go to the hotel at Finleyville, and I shall take the little olives with me." He smiled unpleasantly at Mr. Pierce, whose face did not relax.

He walked jauntily to the door and turned, flourishing the bottle. "The land of the free and the home of the brave!" he sneered, raising the bottle in the air. Standing jeering in the doorway, he bowed to Miss Patty and Mr. Pierce, and put an olive into his mouth.

But instantly he made a terrible face, and clapped a hand just in front of his left ear. He stood there a moment, his face distorted—then he darted into the night, and I never saw him again.

"Mumps!" Doctor Barnes ejaculated, and stood staring after him from the steps.

CHAPTER XXX

LET GOOD DIGESTION

There was no one left but Miss Patty. As she started out past him with a crimson spot in each cheek Mr. Pierce put his hand on her arm. She hesitated, and he closed the door on Doctor Barnes and put his back against it. I had just time to slip back into the pantry and shut myself in.

For a minute there wasn't a sound. Then—

"I told you I should come," Miss Patty said, in her haughtiest manner. "You need not trouble to be disagreeable."

"Disagreeable!" he repeated. "I am abject!"

"I don't understand," she said. "But you needn't explain. It really does not matter."

"It matters to me. I had to do this to-night. I promised you I would make good, and if I had let this pass—Don't you see, I couldn't let it go."

"You can let me go, now."

"Not until I have justified myself to you."

"I am not interested."

I heard him take a step or two toward her.

"I don't quite believe that," he said in a low tone. "You were interested in what I said here this afternoon."

"I didn't hear it."

"None of it?"

"Not—not all."

"I spoke, you remember, about your sister, and about Dick—" he paused. I could imagine her staring at him in her wide-eyed way.

"You never mentioned them!" she said scornfully and stopped. He laughed, a low laugh, boyish and full of triumph.

"Ah!" he said. "So you DID hear! I'm going to say it again, anyhow. I love you, Patty. I'm—I'm mad for you. I've loved you hopelessly for so long that to-night, when there's a ray of hope, I'm—I'm hardly sane. I—"

"Please!" she said.

"I love you so much that I waken at night just to say your name, over and over, and when dawn comes through the windows—"

"You don't know what you are saying!" she said wildly. "I am—still—"

"I welcome the daylight," he went on, talking very fast, "because it means another day when I can see you. If it sounds foolish, it's—it's really lots worse than it sounds, Patty."

The door opened just then, and Doctor Barnes' voice spoke from the step.

"I say," he complained, "you needn't—"

"Get out!" Mr. Pierce said angrily, and the door slammed. The second's interruption gave him time, I think, to see how far he'd gone, and his voice, when he spoke again, was not so hopeful.

"I'm not pleading my cause," he said humbly, "I know I haven't any cause. I have nothing to offer you."

"You said this afternoon," Miss Patty said softly, "that you could offer me the—the kind of love that a woman could be proud of."

She finished off with a sort of gasp, as if she was shocked at herself. I was so excited that my heart beat a tatoo against my ribs, and without my being conscious of it, as you may say, the pantry door opened about an inch and I found myself with an eye to the crack.

They were standing facing each other, he all flushed and eager and my dear Miss Patty pale and trembly. But she wasn't shy. She was looking straight into his eyes and her blessed lips were quivering.

"How can you care?" she asked, when he only stood and looked at her. "I've been such a—such a selfish beast!"

"Hush!" He leaned toward her, and I held my breath. "You are everything that is best in the world, and I—what can I offer you? I have nothing, not even this sanatorium! No money, no title—"

"Oh, THAT!" she interrupted, and stood waiting. "Well, you—you could at least offer yourself!"

"Patty!"

She went right over to him and put her hands on his shoulders.

"And if you won't," she said, "I'll offer myself instead!"

His arms went around her like a flash at that, and he kissed her. I've seen a good many kisses in my day, the spring-house walk being a sort of lover's lane, but they were generally of the quick-get-away variety. This was different. He just gathered her up to him and held her close, and if she was one-tenth as much thrilled as I was in the pantry she'd be ready to die kissing.

Then, without releasing her, he raised his head, with such a look of victory in his face that I still see it sometimes in my sleep, and his eye caught mine through the crack.

But if I'd looked to see him drop her I was mistaken. He drew her up and kissed her again, but this time on the forehead. And when he'd let her go and she had dropped into a chair and hid her shining face against the back, as if she was ashamed, which she might well be, he stood laughing over her bent head at me.

"Come out, Minnie!" he called. "Come out and hear the good news!"

"Hear!" I said, "I've seen all the news I want."

"Gracious!" Miss Patty said, and buried her head again. But he had reached the shameless stage; a man who is really in love always seems to get to that point sooner or later. He stooped and kissed the back of her neck, and if his hand shook when he pushed in one of her shell hairpins it was excitement and not fright.

"I hardly realize it, Minnie," he said. "I don't deserve her for a minute."

"Certainly not," I said.

"He does." Miss Patty's voice smothered. Then she got up and came over to me.

"There is going to be an awful fuss, Minnie," she said. "Think of Aunt Honoria—and Oskar!"

"Let them fuss!" I said grandly. "If the worst comes, you can spend your honeymoon in the shelter-house. I'm so used to carrying meals there now that it's second nature."

And at that they both made for me, and as Mr. Pierce kissed me Doctor Barnes opened the door. He stood for a moment, looking queer and wild, and then he slammed the door and we heard him stamping down the steps.

Mr. Pierce had to bring him back.

Well, that's all there is to it. The place filled up and stayed filled, but not under Mr. Pierce. Mr. Jennings said ability of his kind was wasted there, once the place was running, and set him to building a railroad somewhere or other, with him and Miss Patty living in a private car, and he carrying a portable telephone with him so he can talk to her every hour or so. Mr. Dick and his wife are running the sanatorium, or think they are. Doctor Barnes is the whole place, really. Mr. Jennings was so glad to have Miss Patty give up the prince and send him back home, after he'd been a week in the hotel at Finleyville looking as if his face would collapse if you stuck a pin in it—Mr. Jennings was so happy, not to mention having worked off his gout at the wood-pile, that he forgave the Dickys without any trouble, and even went out and had a meal with them in the shelter-house before they moved in, with Mr. Dick making the coffee.

I miss the spring, as I said at the beginning. It is hard to teach an old dog new tricks, but with Miss Patty happy, and with Doctor Barnes around—

Thoburn came out the afternoon before he left, just after the rest hour, and showed me how much too loose his waistcoat had become.

"I've lost, Minnie," he confessed. "Lost fifteen pounds and the dream of my life. But I've found something, too."

"What?"

"My waist line!" he said, and threw his chest out.

"You look fifteen years younger," I said, and at that he came over to me and took my hand.

"Minnie," he said, "maybe you and I haven't always agreed, but I've always liked you, Minnie—always."

"Thanks," I said, taking my hand away.

"You've got all kinds of spirit," he said. "You've saved the place, all right. And if you—if you tire of this, and want another home, I've got one, twelve rooms, center hall, tiled baths, cabinet mantels—I'd be good to you, Minnie. The right woman could do anything with me."

When I grasped what he meant, I was staggered.

"I'm sorry," I explained, as gently as I could. "I'm—I'm going to marry Doctor Barnes one of these days."

He stared at me. Then he laughed a little and went toward the door.

"Barnes!" he said, turning. "Another redhead, by gad! Well, I'll tell you this, young woman, you're red, but he's redder. Your days for running things to suit yourself are over."

"I'm glad of it," I retorted. "I want to be managed myself for a change. Somebody," I said, "who won't be always thinking how he feels, unless it's how he feels toward me."

"Bah! He'll bully you."

"'It's human nature to like to be bullied,'" I quoted. "And I guess I'm not afraid. He's healthy and a healthy man's never a crank."

"A case of yours for health, eh?" he said, and held out his hand.

THE END

Made in the USA
Middletown, DE
28 September 2018